DANGER COVE

www.dangercovemysteries.com

DANGER COVE BOOKS

Secret of the Painted Lady
Murder and Mai Tais
Death by Scones
Four-Patch of Trouble
Deadly Dye and a Soy Chai
Killer Closet Case
Tree of Life and Death
A Killing in the Market (short story)
Killer Colada
Passion, Poison & Puppy Dogs
A Novel Death
Robbing Peter to Kill Paul
Sinister Snickerdoodles
Heroes and Hurricanes
A Death in the Flower Garden
Divas, Diamonds & Death
A Slaying in the Orchard
A Secret in the Pumpkin Patch
Deadly Dirty Martinis
A Poison Manicure & Peach Liqueur
Not-So-Bright Hopes (short story)
Tequila Trouble

BOOKS BY NICOLE LEIREN

Danger Cove Cocktail Mysteries:
Heroes and Hurricanes
Deadly Dirty Martinis
Tequila Trouble

TEQUILA TROUBLE

a Danger Cove Cocktail mystery

Nicole Leiren &
Elizabeth Ashby

TEQUILA
TROUBLE

CHAPTER ONE

———

"Lilly, you must promise me two things."

I grabbed the second empty glass of tequila sunrise from in front of Danger Cove's newest celebrity. "What's that, Agnes?"

Her red curls bounced as she balanced her chin on one hand, her elbow sliding dangerously close to the edge of the bar. "First and most important, you must promise to never, ever run out of my brand of tequila."

Mandi, my best friend forever (BFF) and head waitress here at Smugglers' Tavern, brought an order up to the bar. She smiled indulgently at Agnes. "Miss Thermopolis, Tsunatka tequila is over three hundred dollars a bottle. You're the only one who can afford that brand, so not much of a chance we'll run out."

Agnes sighed heavily before sitting up straight. "I'm no longer Miss Thermopolis."

Mandi's face blushed bright red, almost matching the shade of her hair. "My apologies. I keep forgetting you got married on the cruise ship." Mandi frowned. "I don't even know what percentage of people get married at sea."

Deciding to rescue Mandi, I handed her the drinks for her order and smiled. "Then you'll have something new to research on your day off."

My comment returned both her smile and hue of her cheeks to their normal state. "You're right. Thanks, Boss. You know how I'm always looking for info to feed my inner trivia monster. This should be fun."

It was true. Mandi had an unending love for all things trivia. Her knowledge of random facts had come in handy both on a personal and professional level for me over the past year.

This was especially important since Hope Foster, owner of Smugglers' Tavern, had left me in charge while she was off exploring the world with her English love, Harvey. She was scheduled to return from her travels soon though. To be honest, I'd spent at least a few sleepless nights wondering where I'd fit into the master plan once that happened.

Regardless of what my role might or might not be once she returned, I was certain Hope wouldn't appreciate me being called "Boss" once she'd returned. Besides, I really enjoyed calling *her* "Boss Lady," even though she hated it. Turning from future concerns and focusing on the present, I rolled my eyes at Mandi and teased, "I'm the only boss you've had, so that's not much of a compliment."

Mandi's good nature came through, and she laughed as she grabbed the tray of drinks. "I'll give you the stats on bosses over ice cream on Sunday."

"That girl loves her trivia and random facts, doesn't she?" Agnes mused as she pointed to the expensive bottle of tequila and gestured for another.

"That she does." I started making the drink, but decided to chat Agnes up a little to increase the space between her beverages. Normally, two was her limit, but from the way she'd been acting since she'd arrived a little while ago, I'd bet she pre-gamed with a few of her own before coming in. "I have some trivia for you. Ready?"

"Do I have a choice?" Agnes chuckled.

"Consider it an exchange for another drink. I'll even toss in a ride home for you. I bet I can sweet talk Tanner into giving you a lift."

Agnes grinned and let her gaze glide over all the envious patrons, who, no doubt, were whispering behind her back, to take in my *not-boyfriend* and chief of security here at the tavern, Tanner Montgomery. To clarify, I only went out on dates with Tanner, and he only went out with me, but labels like *boyfriend* implied commitment and only complicated matters. That complication was something Tanner and I had been discussing more and more the closer he got to his graduation from college.

Tanner must have sensed our gazes as he served up that toothpaste-white smile at both of us and waved. So darn cute, he was. Agnes waved back and then returned her attention to me. "As much as I love that cherry red Mustang of his, I'm fine to get myself home. I may be rich, but I still prefer to drive myself."

She might be rich, thanks to her recent lottery win, but I took my job seriously, and if she needed a ride home, I'd make sure she got one. That was just how we bartenders rolled...well, at least this one. Ready to change the subject, I checked on the other patrons and then finished mixing Agnes's drink. "So what was the second thing you wanted me to promise you?"

"She wants you to promise to never buy a lottery ticket." Local reporter Duncan Pickles and author of the article that had shed a little fame light on Danger Cove, along with Agnes and me, slid onto the wooden stool next to her.

I offered up the obligatory smile. "Your usual?"

He nodded and returned his attention to Agnes. Fine with me. Duncan hadn't been one of my favorite people when I first arrived in Danger Cover a little over a year ago, and not much had happened to change that. Unlike my rock-and-roll, spotlight-seeking father, I was content to hang out in the shadows. Duncan's article about Lady Luck lavishing her attention on Agnes with the lotto win and on me with my surprise inheritance had pushed us both right into the center ring of the circus. It was amazing how many "charitable" organizations you learned about once people realized you'd stumbled upon your pot of gold without the trouble of chasing the rainbow. Agnes had escaped the influx of potential pursuers who either wanted her money or her hand in matrimony as a way of getting to the money by going on a Caribbean cruise.

Well, she'd managed one out of two. Guess that wasn't too bad.

I mixed Duncan's drink and placed it in front of him. "Eight fifty."

Duncan smiled at Agnes, "Would you mind?"

The smile on her face tightened, but held its shape. "Of course. Now run along and play—the adults need to talk."

He had the decency to look slightly abashed, but took the drink and left without even a thank-you. Jerk. I shook my head. "You better hope he doesn't write an article about your generosity at the bar, or you'll be picking up everyone's tab."

Agnes downed her drink. "I won over ten million dollars after taxes. I have more money than I'll ever know what to do with. I could buy drinks for everyone in town, tourists included, every night for a year and still be fine."

"That still doesn't make it right."

Agnes ignored my assessment and pointed to the bottle of tequila. "You promised me some useless trivia about tequila."

"Right. Do you know how many different brands of tequila there are?" Hanging around Mandi must be rubbing off on me.

"Two."

"Two? Agnes, you know that can't be right."

"Not for nuttin', but she's right." Freddie, our busboy and transplant from New York, brought over a clean rack of glasses for me.

Agnes laughed. "Tell her, Freddie."

He set the rack down and pointed to the bottle Agnes had been enjoying her libations from for the last hour or so. "There's her brand," he said. Then he pointed to the other tequilas sitting on the shelf. "Then there's not her brand. When you add those up, you get two."

Not only were her red curls bouncing, Agnes's entire body was jiggling with her laughter. Freddie was funny, but not *that* funny. This was definitely tequila-tainted amusement. "When the boy is right, he's right."

Freddie's bangs fell over his face as he lowered his head in embarrassment. "Thanks, Mrs. Iglesias."

Agnes lifted her hands in the air. "Not only right, but smart. Keep this one around, Lilly."

Freddie noticed some people leaving and used that as an opportunity to make his exit.

I gave Agnes another drink. "This one comes with a ride home, okay?"

She shrugged, and the levity left her as quickly as it had come. "What if I don't want to go home?"

"Oh, come on. The honeymoon can't be over yet."

"Pfft, it would have to start in order to have an ending."

"You want to talk about it?" Bartending 101: when people wanted to talk, you needed to listen.

After a long, slow sip, she finally answered. "Rico has been acting strangely since we got home. On the ship he said and did everything right." She lifted her left hand to admire the rock adorning her ring finger. "But from the moment he slipped this four-carat emerald-cut diamond ring on my finger and I said *I do*, he's been a changed man—and not in a good way."

It wasn't surprising. Since the article, there'd been any number of men who'd come seeking either my hand in marriage or Agnes's. They weren't picky. They just wanted to attach themselves to our fortunes. Because the size of her bank account was about ten times the size of mine, she'd had to contend with them much more than I had. Besides, Tanner had done a pretty good job of dissuading my would-be-suitors. Have I mentioned how I like it when he goes all caveman protector on me? "I'm really sorry, Agnes. Maybe he's just having a tough time adjusting. Where is he from originally?"

"Seattle," she scoffed. "Since that's only an hour away, I don't see that as a big adjustment for him. I've tried to get him to open up about what might be bothering him, but his lips are sealed."

"Maybe it's married life he needs adjusting to?" I was grasping at plastic straws in the condiment bin, but I was trying for my newest friend to find some meaning other than the obvious.

Agnes flipped her hair as she huffed. "I suppose you're right, but I'm making an effort to adjust too. It's not like I've been married before." She crooked her finger to bring me in closer. "He doesn't even like tequila. Honestly, Lilly. What kind of man doesn't like tequila? Or more to the point, how could *I* have married a man who doesn't like tequila?"

I managed to hold my sassy retort about the possibility of her consuming too much tequila prior to her saying *yes*. She didn't want or need to hear that right now. Before I could manage a sass-free response, she continued. "He's been acting very strangely the last couple of days. Very anxious."

She grabbed my hands and held them tightly. "That's the second thing I want you to promise me."

"What's that?"

"Promise me you'll never get married. It's not worth it, trust me." She released me and held up her hand to admire the diamond before grinning. "Well, this at least makes it more tolerable. Isn't it gorgeous?"

It could choke a horse. Again, not what Agnes wanted to hear. "Beautiful."

About that time Tara, my head chef, busted through the kitchen doors. "Oh. Em. Gee. I can't believe it!"

Agnes managed to tear her gaze away from the block of gleaming ice and smiled at her. "Can't believe what, dearie?"

My typically cool, calm, collected culinary genius vibrated with excitement. She looked like she was going to burst. I prayed it was a good burst and not an I-can't-take-this-anymore-and-I'm-leaving-you-on-a-Saturday-night burst. Yeah, those were a thing. I'd had them before. Not since coming to Danger Cove, but during my time in New Orleans. For the official record, they were not fun.

"He's coming here—tonight!" The pitch of her voice registered on the scale as a squeal of delight amplified by an element of elation.

Her admission didn't help us at all. "Who's coming here?"

"Chef Jonathan!"

I still didn't have a clue.

Agnes jumped in and saved me from asking the obvious question. "Who is Chef Jonathan?"

I felt like we were playing a game of twenty questions, and I was totally on the losing team.

Tara inhaled deeply then exhaled slowly. "Sorry. It's just...I...I've had the biggest crush on him since he appeared on the cover of *Haute Cuisine*. Chef Jonathan Patterson is *the* hottest chef right now, and he's coming to Danger Cove."

Mandi joined the conversation. "My mom reads that magazine. She Googled him. He's been wowing the critics with his unique combinations while still managing to appease your average, everyday eater. Apparently, that's quite impressive."

What I knew about critics and unique combinations wouldn't impress anyone. I used my microwave and toaster oven to prepare any meals I braved at home. My goal was enough nourishment to last me until Clara or Tara fed me during the workday. "He sounds like a great chef, but he'd have to be pretty fantastic to make me want his food more than our chefs' here."

Before Tara could soak up my compliment, the front door opened, and a man of medium height and build, with dark hair and a five o'clock shadow stepped through.

Tara grabbed my arm. "It's him!" Her urgent whisper was followed by her body swaying back and forth as she stared in his direction.

Agnes cackled. "She's swooning. I love it. Youthful infatuation is such a fun thing. I miss that."

Jonathan strode confidently up to the bar. He looked at me and then at Agnes. "Just the two ladies I came here to see."

CHAPTER TWO

———

I had no idea which two of the three ladies standing in front of him he wanted to see. Even a greater mystery was, aside from Tara, why he would want to see Agnes or me. At the end of the day, it didn't matter. He was a customer, and it was my job to make him feel welcome. "Hi, and welcome to Smugglers' Tavern. Can I get you something to drink? I would also like to introduce you to my head chef, Tara, as I'm certain she's your biggest fan."

I turned to gesture Tara up to the bar, but she'd disappeared. I shrugged and smiled. "The kitchen must have called. I'll be sure to introduce her before you leave. Her special tonight is the roasted chicken, and if the patrons' compliments are any indication, it's a big hit."

He did a quick perusal of the bar area and the listed specials before his gaze returned to me. "I would love a tequila sunrise and the roasted chicken with chef's-choice vegetables." He gestured to the seat next to Agnes. "May I sit here?"

Agnes batted her eyelashes and gave him a sparkling smile. "Honey, you can sit anywhere you like." She then turned to me. "Lilly, put his first drink on my tab."

I shook my head and chuckled. "Sure thing, Mrs. Iglesias."

There might have been a bit of sass in my stressing the *missus* part of my reply. Agnes and I were friends, which meant I could tease her a little bit. I made Chef Jonathan his drink (using the cheaper tequila) and then headed to the kitchen to put in his order and check on Tara.

Reassured Tara was just nervous about meeting her hero in person, I exited the kitchen doors.

Immediately, Agnes waved at me. "Lilly, you have to come over here. He won't tell me why he's here until we're both present and accounted for."

They both must have missed the part where I was working and had to tend to all the patrons, not just one or two. "Give me a minute to make sure everyone has a fresh drink, and then I'll be with you."

"Take your time, Miss Waters. I don't plan on leaving until I get a chance to talk to both of you."

Wow, okay, now it was all starting to make sense. You take a Miss Waters and add in a Mrs. Iglesias, and that equaled Chef Jonathan looking for one of the two *M*s—marriage or money. Since Agnes was married and I had no intention of walking down the aisle, that translated into him simply asking for money. The question would be what story he would weave to convince us to divest our bank accounts of the cash.

Great. Just what I needed on a busy Saturday night.

By the time I made it back to Agnes and Jonathan, I could swear he had Agnes swooning, just as Tara had been earlier. Maybe I was missing something about him. Don't get me wrong—he was nice looking, but definitely not swoon worthy. Now Tanner...he occasionally warranted a slight swoon. "Okay, you both have me for at least three to five minutes before I'll need to check on everyone."

"You're very good at what you do, Miss Waters."

I needed to put a stop to the *Miss* thing right now. "Lilly is fine."

Agnes grinned. "Told you."

Jonathan blushed from her tease. "Lilly it is then. As I was saying, you're very good at what you do. Agnes has been filling me in on how you've been taking care of things at the tavern while the owner is away."

"Thank you. She taught me well, and I have a great team."

"You didn't mention how humble she was, Agnes."

"Well, Agnes and I haven't been friends for that long, so she still has a few things to learn about me, I guess." I had to bite my tongue to keep from mentioning that he'd used up at least one, if not two, of his precious minutes buttering me up. I wanted him to get to the point. *So I can say no and get back to the business at hand.*

"Right, you met when you did the interview for that newspaper article."

Agnes jumped into the conversation. "Actually, I met Lilly last year when her mother was being held for questioning for murder."

"Agnes!"

Jonathan laughed. "Everyone has secrets, Lilly. Some more costly than others. I'm sure your mother was found not guilty."

I glared at Agnes, who was clearly amused by my aggravation. "For the official record, my mother was never charged, just questioned. She was released, and the real killer was apprehended." I left out the other details about my involvement in that whole matter. I wanted this conversation to be over as soon as possible.

Jonathan nodded. "I've done my research. I always thoroughly vet potential investors before I approach them. Can't have anything tarnishing the polished silver of my reputation, can I?"

And there it was—the reason for his visit and the *why* we should get out our checkbooks. I breathed a small sigh of relief he wasn't even going to try the matrimony angle.

Agnes, on the other hand, might be disappointed he wasn't at least going to *try* that angle with her. I swear she was batting her eyelashes at him as she talked. I couldn't be sure how much of that was tequila inspired and how much was just Agnes being…well, Agnes.

"I don't mean to be rude, but it's a Saturday night, and as you can see, we're very busy. Based on the not-so-subtle hints you've dropped, you're here to ask for money." If Agnes weren't so distracted by his charm, she'd see his intent as clearly as I did. He was just one in a long line that had arrived in Danger Cove looking for a handout. I really should throttle Duncan Pickles for sharing our stories. If Agnes wanted to announce *her* newfound wealth to the world, that was fine. One of these days I'd learn to stop succumbing to peer pressure. I preferred to live a quiet and simple life. Chef Jonathan represented neither of those.

He had the decency to look taken aback by my statement. "Lilly, I would never ask you for money. Well, certainly not the two hundred thousand I'm seeking from Agnes. I understand your inheritance was less sizeable than Agnes's lottery win. I'm looking for fifty thousand from you, but the important question is, what am I offering you?"

First he insulted my bank account, and then he wanted to play twenty questions. This should be good. "Okay, I'll bite. What exactly are you offering me in exchange for my paltry fifty grand?"

His chest expanded more than a puffer fish's. "What I'm offering you is the opportunity of a lifetime."

Agnes leaned closer to Chef Jonathan. "Do tell us more. I live for opportunities."

I swear her smile dripped with syrup—it was so sweet. The question was, opportunities for what?...but I'd save that question for when Agnes and I were alone.

Jonathan put his hand on Agnes's shoulder and turned the charm up another notch. "I'm expanding my empire by opening a premier restaurant in San Francisco. It will be unlike any other restaurant in town." His pride was evident, and arrogance oozed from every pore. "Of course, with my name on the door, success is guaranteed regardless."

One corner of my mouth quirked up in an effort to keep my eyes from rolling. I was pretty sure there was an invisible connection between the two expressions. "Of course."

Agnes leaned back and crossed her arms, a dangerous gleam in her eyes. "Well, I'm not convinced. I, for one, have never had the privilege of eating cuisine you've prepared. You may be famous in other areas of the country, but before I invest my money, I would need you to demonstrate your expertise."

Jonathan's ego balloon deflated an inch or two, which was highly entertaining. I liked that she aggravated people around her equally, regardless of status. Maybe that was part of the reason she and Rico were already on a rocky road.

"As much as I would love to, Agnes, I fear I have no place to demonstrate for you. And..." He winked at her. "I didn't come to Danger Cove for the sole purpose of seeking investment capital." He looked directly at me. "I came with the intention of convincing Lilly to come and work for me. I want her to run the restaurant."

I fought the urge to use one of the plastic swords in the garnish bin to clean out my ears. I couldn't have heard him right. "I'm sorry. What did you say?"

"I want you to leave Smugglers' Tavern and be the manager of my newest venture."

The world stopped for just a moment as I contemplated his offer. One part of my psyche reminded me this was Mr. Charm, and he would say or do anything to get what he wanted. You didn't get to be the top dog and as well respected as he apparently was without knowing how to appeal to the ego of others. The other part reminded me that I'd been worried about how I would fit in once Hope returned. Maybe this was the universe showing me a new path? I'd need to ask Ruby. Not only was she Hope's best friend, but her life experience and the way she was in tune with the universe had also provided solid counsel to me on several occasions. My goal was to be at least half as wise as she was, and if I could manage to be as toned, tanned, and tough as she was too, life would be good.

Agnes turned serious. "Lilly being involved would definitely sweeten the pot, but I simply must taste your cooking before I make a sizeable investment."

Score one for Agnes. She had Jonathan drooling at her use of the word *sizeable*. The swoonee had become the swooner. Those probably weren't words, but they were working for me in this moment.

Jonathan pulled his lower lip into his mouth and chewed thoughtfully before answering. "My reputation should speak for itself. I'd be happy to host both you and Lilly at my restaurant in Los Angeles."

I shook my head. "I can't make the trip. Sorry. With Hope away, I'm in charge. I take my responsibility very seriously."

Julie, the young woman who got my job at Charlie's Cove Restaurant and my former apartment when she moved into town was also sitting at the bar. She must've overheard part of our conversation. "I'm sure Uncle Charlie would let you use his kitchen tomorrow morning. Smugglers' is open, but we're closed."

Agnes clapped her hands together and sat up straighter. "Brilliant! You can showcase your talents for us, and then we can discuss business on Monday when Lilly is off work."

Jonathan shook his head. "I'd planned to leave town on Monday. I'll have to see if my schedule can be adjusted."

"I'm confident you'll find a way." Agnes grinned as she closed in on her victory.

Small beads of perspiration had formed on Jonathan's chiseled jaw. Why was he so nervous?

About that time, Tara brought out his food. Her hands only trembled slightly as she put the food in front of him. "Here you go, chef. I hope you like it."

He held up his finger to indicate she should wait. He couldn't see it, but I noticed her foot tapping a mile a minute. I knew she had nothing to worry about, but right now the only confirmation she would hear would be from her idol. He cut into the chicken and lifted the piece to his nose to inhale the seasoning and spice. A moment later, the bite finally disappeared behind those gleaming incisors. If the man did everything as slowly as he chewed, it was a good thing someone else would be running his restaurant, as people would die of starvation waiting for him to finish a meal.

Finally, his eyes closed as he murmured his approval. "Perfecto. Well done, young lady."

Forget swooning. Tara practically melted right in front of me. Her mouth opened, but nothing came out. I decided to rescue her. "She says thank you. We're glad you enjoyed that first bite. Just wait until you consume the whole meal."

He reached across the bar and clasped Tara's forearm. "Say you'll be my sous chef tomorrow when I prepare a meal for these two ladies."

Tara finally found her voice. "I always work with my sister. Can she come too?"

The pomp returned to Jonathan's circumstance. "Of course she can. If she's part of the team that created this savory selection, I would be honored to share the kitchen with both of you."

"Great. Thank you! I'll let her know."

He turned to Julie. "If you'll double-check with your uncle…"

She held up her phone to show the text message exchange. "He's good to go. You can get in there by seven in the morning. Serve breakfast by eight. That way everyone can be here by the time they need to get ready for opening. I'll even help you clean up."

Agnes clapped her hands together. "It's all set then." She looked at me. "I have a feeling tomorrow is going to be a day that will change our lives forever."

CHAPTER THREE

———

When I arrived at Charlie's Cove the next morning, Agnes and Rico were already there. I'd brought Tanner with me as we'd had precious little quality time together lately due to how busy we'd been with the tavern and his finals schedule. It was hard to believe he was graduating in just a few short weeks.

"Good morning, Lilly. Tanner. Good to see both of you." Agnes appeared much happier to be here than her husband.

I nodded. "Morning, Agnes. Hi, Rico. Good to see you again."

Rico stood, took my hand, and kissed its back. "Good morning yourself, beautiful. My apologies for not dining in your fine establishment more often. I will remedy that right away."

I wasn't sure who was more aggravated by Rico's actions, Agnes or Tanner. Tension radiated off both. I took it for what it was…a player being a player. Just because he'd put a ring on Agnes's finger didn't mean he could stop being who he was—at least not for a while. It was no surprise Agnes had been attracted to him. He stood about six foot tall with coal black, close-cropped hair and a five o'clock shadow that had no regard for what time of day or night it was. It worked for him.

Tanner's blond hair, ocean blue eyes, and lean build worked for me. Which was why Rico's flirtations rolled off me faster than tequila slid down Agnes's throat. I smiled at Rico and grabbed Tan's hand while ignoring the caveman vibes emanating from every muscle in his body. Maybe if Agnes and Rico came to Smugglers' together more often, I could learn more about their relationship and try to help my friend. "That sounds great. I look forward to seeing both of you there."

About that time, Clara, twin sister to Tara and her right hand in the kitchen, came out. "Lilly, can I see you for a moment?"

Her serious demeanor put me on high alert. "Sure."

"In private."

I squeezed Tan's hand. "Be right back."

Clara and I moved to the opposite side of the seating area. "Is everything alright?"

She crossed her arms and scowled. "No, everything is not alright. He's supposed to be *the* chef of the hour, yet Tara and I are doing all the work. And..." She stressed the word by drawing it out and lacing it with irritation. "When he actually does do something, it's totally wrong. When Tara tries to clarify his intent, he laughs and says he was testing her. I swear, Lilly, you'd think we were the top chefs rather than him."

While understandable that she was frustrated, her irritation level seemed incongruous with what she'd told me so far. "Maybe he's trying to teach you both? I'm not sure. I don't know how things are done in a kitchen. I never spend any quality time in the Smugglers' or in my own, for that matter."

Clara leaned in and lowered her voice to a whisper. "Oh, he's testing Tara, alright. He said he wanted to hire her to be the head chef in his new restaurant."

My stomach, along with any appetite I'd brought with me, dropped to the wooden floor of Charlie's dining area. While he'd mentioned that he wanted me to manage his new restaurant, it hadn't been an official job offer. I saw it more as him offering an incentive to invest the fifty grand he'd mentioned first. Despite his supposed stellar reputation, even if it were an official offer, I wouldn't take it—at least I didn't think so. Gram taught me to never say never. But Hope had been so good to me. I'd made friends, found my family roots, and had Tanner in my corner. No fancy-shmancy restaurant in San Francisco was going to seduce me with its siren song regardless of how beautiful the music might be. "What did she say? Did he offer you a job too?"

"She's too busy gushing over him. I'm getting sick. Can we just leave? Please?"

I'd never seen Clara this upset. Since I'd known them, Clara and Tara had done everything together, even finished each other's sentences. The fact that Jonathan wanted to separate them and that Tara hadn't immediately shut him down...not good for one half of the dynamic duo. "Of course, we can. Let's grab Tanner, and we'll leave."

We walked back to the table and found Agnes and Rico in a whispered, but heated, discussion. This morning wasn't going well at all. "We're going to leave, Agnes. I think you and Rico should come too. This just doesn't feel right."

Rico stood. "I agree. I want to get out of here. I only came to make my bride happy."

Agnes crossed her arms. "She will only remain happy if we stay and enjoy the meal that's being prepared for us."

Clara interjected, "Well, I'm leaving. I don't want any part of this." Even though her words were strong, the moisture gathering in the corners of her eyes gave her away.

Her emotional distress broke through to Agnes. Clara and Tara's childhood home, and where their parents still lived, was next door to Agnes's house. She nodded. "Okay, dear, no need for tears. We'll go and get this all sorted out."

Just as we all stood, Tara came out with a tray of drinks. "Hi, everyone. Please take your seats. Agnes, we have a blood orange margarita for you. There's green tea with honey for Lilly. I wasn't sure what the rest of you would like, so I have some options for you to choose from."

The earnest expression on Tara's face set a battle to raging inside Agnes, if the way she looked from one twin to the other was any indication. I didn't blame her. I didn't think I'd be able to choose between the two of them. We'd never had to until Chef Jonathan showed up.

Wanting to end the stalemate, I took Clara's hand. "You and your sister both worked hard on the meal. Why don't we eat it, and then we can talk through everything? Will that be okay?"

Clara's chin dropped perceptibly as she wiped the errant tears. "You stay and eat, but I want to leave. I'm not feeling well."

I gave her a hug, my way of trying to hold her heart together until we could find a way to do more than a patch job on it. "Do you want to take today off?" I whispered as I squeezed a little tighter.

She didn't answer, but from the direction of her head movement, I interpreted her response as a no. "I'm going to go to the park for a little bit to clear my head, but then I'll go to the tavern and get started on prep."

"Okay. I'll be there as soon as I can. Call my cell if you need anything."

Before she could leave, a blonde woman came in the restaurant. I spoke up right away. "I'm sorry. The restaurant is closed. This is a private event." The last thing we needed was a stranger to witness all this drama.

The woman completely ignored me. "Where is he?"

"Where is who?" I felt another round of twenty questions starting.

She ignored me—again. This time her gaze traveled the room, resting for a moment on each person. As the woman completed her survey, Clara explained to me in a soft voice, "That's Allyson Seavers. She and Jonathan were an item until a month or so ago when they had a very public breakup." She leaned closer to me and lowered her voice. "The tabloids said she cheated on him."

Okay, never mind about our drama. This woman was bringing enough of her own baggage to fill Samsonite's new fall line. When her gaze landed on Rico, fire blazed. "What in the hell are you doing here? You low-life sack of…"

"Hi, I don't think we've met. I'm Tanner Montgomery."

Tanner, accustomed to dealing with rowdy patrons at the tavern, stepped in to play my favorite role: knight in white cotton.

Allyson stopped long enough to give Tanner a quizzical glance. Maybe she was weighing what level of politeness she should extend to him or whether to simply ignore him and resume her attack on Rico. Either way, the pause would hopefully de-escalate this situation.

Oblivious to the action unfolding, Jonathan emerged from the kitchen with a tray full of food. "Brunch is served. We have cinnamon raisin bread with custard and fresh berries and artichoke scrambled eggs benedict. I wanted to make you some of my signature recipes, but I fear that I was unable to secure the supplies in the short time that I had. I will also be serving—"

"Jonathan, I need to speak with you." Allyson interrupted his menu mantra.

He ignored her statement—guess two could play at that game—and began placing the dishes in front of us.

Allyson continued despite his silence. "I made a mistake. I still love you, and I intend to fight for you...for us. I'm sorry."

"As you can see, I'm very busy."

Ouch. Score one on the hurt card for Jonathan. To her credit, Allyson held it together. She looked at Rico. "For the official record, I hate you and rue the day I ever laid eyes on you."

Rico chuckled. "It was more than your eyes, baby."

Allyson lunged toward him, but Tanner was lightning fast and got in between them. "You should probably go now."

His voice was calm, low, and sent a spark of sexy right to my core. I needed to get a grip on my hormones before I added a whole different level of drama to this scene.

Allyson lifted her hands in surrender and stepped back. "I'm leaving." As she got to the door, she turned to Jonathan. "This isn't over. You and I both know it."

She'd no sooner left than Clara stepped toward the door. "I'm leaving too." With one last heart-wrenching look at Tara, she disappeared.

Tara had the decency to look a little dejected too. Definitely needed to make fixing this a top priority when we got back to the tavern. Wanting that to be sooner than later, I lifted my fork. "Bon appétit, everyone."

Abysmal emotional energy settled in the room heavier than a wet blanket. The food was good, though if I was being totally honest, Tara and Clara's food at the tavern was just as good. Maybe my taste buds favored meals made by friends? Or it was possible all the negativity of the morning erased my desire to try anything new. My poor stomach was used to microwave meals.

Once finished, Agnes smiled. "Thank you, chefs, for the meal. Jonathan, I'll give you an answer in the next twenty-four hours."

Jonathan nodded. "Thank you for your time and consideration."

Before the chef could question me, I interjected, "Tara, why don't you and Tanner head back to the tavern to start prepping? If that's okay, I'll stay to help clear the table."

Rico stood. "Agnes, don't you have some things to take care of at the house? I'll help clear the table as well."

Jonathan retreated to the kitchen, followed closely by Rico. I noticed he hadn't bothered to pick up even a glass or fork. Some help he was going to be.

Tanner kissed me on the cheek. "You sure you're okay here with those two?"

"I'll be fine." I returned his kiss, but instead of his cheek, I found those soft lips of his. Though the uncertainty of the future—of our future—remained, I was glad he'd be here full time in the area once he graduated. At least I hoped he would. He'd indicated he wanted to find a job nearby so he wouldn't be far from where he grew up. Between work at the tavern and schoolwork, the days he spent here on the weekends didn't offer much in the way of quality time together. "Ice cream at my place tonight?"

His smile melted me where I stood. "I'll bring chocolate sauce."

With that promise, he and Tara left. I started scraping and stacking dishes, anxious to get back to *my* restaurant. I didn't feel at home in Charlie's restaurant—never really had. And I knew there was little chance I'd feel at home in Jonathan's. If his job offer was genuine, I needed to let him down, but wanted to do it easy.

I quietly opened the door to the kitchen when I heard Rico's voice ringing out loud and clear. "I don't know what game you're playing at, but you're not getting one dime of Agnes's money, much less however many hundreds of thousands of dollars you're trying to charm her out of. Stay the hell away from my wife. Are we clear? You'll have to climb over my dead body to get even one penny."

Rico's threat was clear as crystal to me, and I was on the other side of the kitchen. After Clara's departure, Allyson's interruption, and now Rico's hostility, I decided I'd talk to Jonathan later. He was having a very bad day, and I didn't want to add to it. I placed the dishes on the counter and started to back out quietly when Jonathan replied.

"Threats are unnecessary. This is simply business. No need to make things personal, though I'm starting to understand how personal this might be for you."

I had no idea what that meant, but I understood that, personally, I needed to make my exit and leave them to their testosterone exchange. I'd just made it to my bike, parked safely on the other side of the lot, when Rico stormed out of the restaurant. The loose gravel in the parking lot spitted and sputtered a tsunami of debris in my direction as he peeled out and headed toward his side of town.

I'd almost made it back to the tavern when Tanner called me. "Are you stalking me?" I laughed as I answered the phone. "I'm almost there."

He chuckled. "If I were using the stalker app, I'd know that already."

The man had a point. He and I both had an app on our phones that allowed us to track each other via the GPS signal. It provided just the right combination of sweet and stalker to prevent things from being awkward. "Did you miss me?"

"Of course, but that's not why I called. I wanted you to know that your new gardener hasn't shown up for work yet. I'm retrieving some herbs the ladies need to start prep, but thought you should know. There are a few things we still need for today's menu though."

"You get employee of the month for sure."

"As long as the bonus is quality time with the boss, I'm good with that."

"I don't think Harvey would appreciate you getting quality time with Hope," I teased. "Especially not with them traversing the country together."

"Sassy, sassy girl. You know what I mean."

I laughed. "I do. Thanks for covering. I'll deal with him as soon as I get back. Text me the list, and I'll pick up what we need while I'm out."

I reversed direction and headed toward the farmers' market to pick up the items on the list. The extra pedaling gave me time to process everything I'd witnessed between Agnes,

Rico, Allyson, and Jonathan. My curiosity kitties were clawing at me to call Bree, my friend who managed the Ocean View Bed & Breakfast, to see if Allyson was staying there. I'd love to know more about what had happened between her and Rico to cause such animosity. They obviously had history, and from their interaction, it didn't take being in tune with the universe to know it hadn't ended well.

I'd just parked my bike and caught my breath when my cell rang. I answered the call, "Hello?"

"Lilly! It's Agnes." She started coughing and wheezing. "I need you to come over. It's Rico. I think he's dead."

CHAPTER FOUR

———

Agnes's house was, of course, farther away than I wanted it to be. My legs were burning from the pedaling, and I swore to myself for the hundredth—okay thousandth—time that I would find a way to incorporate cardio into my routine. Sleep wasn't necessary, right?

I hoped Agnes had called for an ambulance. Heaven only knew why she'd called me. First aid was barely in my skill sets. If Rico was as serious as she claimed…

As soon as her house came into sight, I hopped off the bike and let it skid to the ground on its own. Hopefully, no damage would come to my sole mode of transportation. I banged on the front door, but no one answered. "Agnes? Agnes! Open the door."

Nothing. The house was eerily quiet. Both Agnes's and Rico's vehicles were in the drive. They had to be home. I ran around to the backyard, shimmying through a part of the privacy fence that had a broken slat. I was sure that was on Agnes's list of things to do with her millions of dollars. Ensuring she was well stocked with premium tequila had taken precedence though. At the rate she'd been imbibing, it would probably be a good use of her money to invest in the Tsunatka Tequila Company. At least then she'd simply be funneling her money from one hand to the other.

The back door was unlocked, so I pulled it open and darted inside. Immediately I could smell noxious fumes. They got stronger as I made my way from the kitchen to the dining room. Tears clouded my eyes, making it hard to see, and inhaling produced an ugly cough. I quickly returned to the part of the kitchen that housed the windows. With a surge of strength, I pried them open, enjoying the availability of some fresh air.

The clean oxygen renewed my resolve, and I headed further into the house to find Rico and Agnes. I'd been here a couple times before. The house was old, certainly not your modern open floor plan that homes are designed with these days. The kitchen had two doors. One led to the dining room, the other to the laundry room and storage area. The dining room was situated between the kitchen and formal living room. Off the dining room was the area where Agnes would spend most of her time. More of a den that housed a desk, recliner, television, and her cats.

After a few quick inhales of the air seeping in through the screen in the windows, I headed through the kitchen and into the dining room. Rico was lying on the other side of the large mahogany table, his perfectly combed dark hair matted near his temple with blood. Not good.

Agnes was closer to the entryway into the living room, cell phone in one hand and surrounded by shards of broken glass. *Dear God, please don't let her be dead too.* A low moan escaped her ruby red lips, snapping me out of this nightmare and into action. Pulling my cell phone from my back pocket, I dialed 9-1-1—just in case Agnes hadn't—and relayed the situation. Confident help was on its way, I moved over to Agnes to help her to her feet. I cast a quick glance at Rico. No way could I move him by myself. Doing a quick mental calculation, I decided the back porch was closer. Once Agnes was standing, I took her hand. "Help me get him out of here."

We each grabbed him under the arm at the shoulder and pulled. Thanks to a mighty infusion of adrenaline, my muscles took on superhero powers. Supergirl better look out. Who needed someone from Krypton when mild-mannered Lilly Waters—born in Las Vegas and raised in Woodstock, New York—was in the room?

A few minutes later, we'd managed to drag him outside and into breathable air. I assumed he was still breathing. Our immediate task done, Agnes dropped into one of the cushioned chairs on the porch.

I rushed to her side. "Are you alright? What happened? If this is a gas leak, we need to get further away from here now!"

Agnes coughed a few times before her gaze darted to Rico. "No gas leak. Oh God, this is all my fault."

"The paramedics are on their way. They will be able to help him far better than you or me."

Agnes went to Rico's side and dropped to her knees. She placed her fingers on his neck and then shook her head. "I've never done this before. I'm not sure if I'm feeling my pulse or his. My heart is racing so fast. Can you check, please?"

I bit my lip, unsure how to break the news to Agnes. "It wouldn't do any good."

"Oh no…do you think…do you know…is he…dead? Is that why you won't check? Oh good Lord."

Gah, this was hard. I grabbed her by both shoulders to get her to focus on me rather than Rico. "Agnes, I need you to listen…" *And not be mad that you called me.* "It won't do any good for me to check for a pulse because I can't even find my own."

She stopped sniffling and turned her wide green gaze fully on me. "What do you mean?"

I wasn't sure how else I could put it. "I mean just what I said. I'm completely inept at finding a pulse."

A giggle emerged—not because what I'd said was funny. No, this was more of an ironic-twist-of-fate giggle that kept her from going totally off the rocker as she processed the information I'd just fed her.

"I need a drink." Her gaze traveled longingly toward the house. "Please, can you grab my bottle of tequila off the dining room table?"

The last thing I wanted to do was go back in the room where the fumes were the strongest. Honestly, I'd just saved her life and maybe Rico's by calling the paramedics. How could she ask me to go back in there for a drink? I think the fumes were still affecting her ability to think rationally. The combination of tequila and fumes might be a more viable explanation. "How about some water?"

Tears welled up in her eyes as she looked at Rico again. "Please?"

Ugh! I was such a sucker for tears. If I ever had kids, it wouldn't take them long to figure out this superhero's kryptonite. "Fine." With one deep inhale of fresh air, I opened the back door and darted through the kitchen and into the dining room. It took less than a second for me to realize there was nothing there. Using what breath I had left, I shut all the doors in the dining room that led to the rest of the house. Once assured there was nothing more I could do, I rejoined Agnes. "There wasn't anything on the table."

A confused look unfolded on her freckled face. "I could've sworn I'd just gotten out a fresh bottle—hadn't even opened it yet. I think the last one is in the liquor cabinet."

Since I didn't see such a cabinet here in the kitchen, that meant it was back in the dining room. Though I understood her need for a drink right now, as this scenario could make anyone want to drink, my lungs were mounting a mighty protest. "Are you sure that's the best thing right now?"

The hazel of her eyes flashed to a brilliant green. "I'm well aware I've been drinking more since my marriage, but can we save the intervention until after I know if my husband is dead or not?"

Before I could retrieve the bottle, a pounding on the front door gave me a reprieve from heading back into the danger zone. I quickly unlocked the fence. No need to slide through the opening this time. I ran to the front of the house to direct the EMTs to where we needed them.

They immediately went to work on Rico to assess his vitals. I was certain they were better at the whole pulse checking than Agnes and I put together.

"What happened?" the woman asked as the man continued working.

Agnes's gaze was locked on Rico, so I shook my head and answered. "I'm not sure. Agnes assures me it wasn't a gas leak, but the fumes are pretty bad."

She nodded and returned to assisting her partner. The grim expression on black shirt number one told me what my fingers to Rico's neck or wrist would not. They didn't even need to say the words. He was dead.

I knew, from my limited experience interacting with ambulance personnel, that they wouldn't give up without a fight. After one look at Agnes, who'd started crying, an action that caused her violent cough to resume, they bolted into what I thought of as Jesus mode. In other words, trying to bring someone back from the dead. It had worked for Lazarus, but I didn't think Rico's chances were good.

One moved the gurney into position while the other came over to check on Agnes. "Are you alright, ma'am?"

Agnes gasped for air as she sobbed and coughed.

Black shirt number two shouted, "We need oxygen over here, stat!"

Before any response could be made, Agnes stood and waved off their concern. "I'm fine. Just distraught. Oxygen won't help that."

The EMT looked at me, and I shrugged. Truly, this was not my area of expertise. The medical field had never been a consideration for this girl. Florence Nightingale had nothing to fear from me taking her place in history.

About that time one of the EMTs who had been dealing with Rico looked up. "Let's get him to the hospital. It looks like he fell and hit his head to me, but..." He shot a quick glance between his partner and then to Agnes. "Do you want me to call another ambulance for you? You can ride with your husband too."

Agnes shook her head. "No need for another ambulance. I'll be fine."

He nodded. "Okay, then if you're coming with us, we need to go."

Her hands started to tremble, and the tears continued their free fall down her cheek. "I can't. I don't do well with things like this."

The EMT looked at me. I nodded and decided to test out my superpower of persuasion. "Agnes, you should go. I'll take care of things here. Plus, your cough sounds nasty. You really should have that checked out." I left out the part about the police being on their way. Agnes wasn't in any shape to deal with them right now. She was barely holding it together.

Agnes nodded. "Okay, I'll ride along in the ambulance. Just don't expect me to do anything."

The woman EMT offered a hint of a smile. "I'm sure my partner and I will be able to handle it. You can be there for moral support."

There was some general commotion as they got Rico and Agnes loaded. Once they were gone, there was just me and the gentle breeze of the late morning. It would've been a beautiful day. Would've been if Rico wasn't really dead—which he was. I might not be able to feel blood pumping through veins, but I could read facial expressions. These medical professionals should never play poker.

Until Agnes called me to let me know what was going on, which I was confident she would, I decided to go back inside and see if there was anything I could do to help. Thankfully, the fumes had either dissipated or the doors were doing their job and keeping the worst of it in the dining room.

I wished I'd had an opportunity to ask Agnes what happened before the ambulance arrived, though I was grateful they'd arrived quickly. I knew the police would be here soon. I was pretty sure it was an automatic thing when the paramedics were called. One of those just-in-case things—whatever that meant.

I grabbed a bottle of water from the refrigerator and sat at her kitchen table. There had been a lot of questions brewing around in my mind since I arrived here. My cell phone buzzed. The caller ID showed it was Agnes. I preferred the "no news is good news" angle right now, but I guess she wanted to share whatever she'd learned. "Hello?"

"We're at the hospital. I'm in the waiting room. I wanted to see if you were still at the house."

"I'm here. Hey, Agnes, before things get crazy again, can I ask you a question?"

She chuckled. "You mean they aren't crazy *still*? But sure, go ahead and ask. It's the least I can do to thank you for helping me…us."

The question branding itself on the front of my brain needed to be asked first. "Why did you call me instead of official help in the first place?" I didn't want to point out that the delay while I pedaled like a madwoman to get over here might have cost Rico his life."

There was a pause and a slight cough. "I meant to call them. You're number nine on my speed dial. When I pressed the number to start the 9-1-1 call, I started coughing and held the button too long. Instead of being able to hit the one key, it dialed you."

I could almost hear the embarrassment in her voice.

"And like a dear, you came right away. Thank you again for that."

I leaned forward in the chair. In my own way, trying to close the distance between us. "That's what friends are for. May I ask you another question?"

There was a pause as I heard her muffled answer to someone at the hospital. After a moment, she answered. "Sorry about that. Ask away."

"If it wasn't a gas leak, what was the cause of the fumes? The smell was incredibly strong—toxic even."

"I don't know, to be honest. I put my ring in a glass to soak in a special cleaning solution I'd just learned about from a fellow DIYer. You know how I like to do things myself."

She was kind of independent, but I'd never taken her for someone who watched the DIY channel, much less have a DIY friend. Learned something new about Agnes today, I guess. I decided to keep the conversation flowing, I'd not argue with her. "Yes, you do. So you made your own special cleaner. Then what?"

"Once I dropped the ring in, I left Rico sitting at the table and went next door to visit Clara and Tara's parents. I wanted to tell them what a great meal the girls had helped prepare this morning." I heard a few sniffles through the connection. "Rico and I had been arguing since he got home. He was adamant that I not invest in Chef Jonathan's venture. I was adamant it was my money to do with as I pleased."

There was a longer pause this time. "All of this because I wanted to clean my ring."

I heard her gasp. "My ring! Lilly, you must find it. I must have dropped it when I passed out. When I realized my solution was the source of the fumes, I tried to get the glass outside while calling for help. The coughing made me drop the glass and…what a mess. Please, Lilly. You have to find the ring. I don't want to worry about that and Rico."

"Okay, okay. Stay calm. I'll look around." Some days being a good, decent person and friend added way too many things to your to-do list. "I'll call you as soon as I find it."

"Thank you so much. I'll be in touch."

I shot off a quick text to Tan and Mandi to let them know why I was running late and asked them to hold down the fort until I could get there. That detail handled, I got down to the business of finding Agnes's ring. How hard could it be? It was large enough to choke a horse, and the gems should nicely reflect off the fancy flashlight on my cell phone.

Thankfully, the fumes had dissipated somewhat when I entered the dining room. Still not pleasant, but not unbreathable anymore. I rotated the beam of light in a back-and-forth pattern, starting at the farthest corner of the room. Square by square, I followed the tiles. The only reflection came when I got to the broken glass. Not wanting to sacrifice my capris or my knees, I located the broom and started to sweep up the shards, when I stopped. If Rico was dead, I was pretty sure it was an accident. But I could just hear Detective Marshall or, as I liked to call him, Detective Pizza Guy berating me for meddling with the scene yet again. In my defense, I called him that because the first time we'd met, he'd tried to get me to confess to something I didn't do in order to get back to his pizza before it got cold.

He'd had valid concerns about my making a mess of the crime scenes in the past. The first time I'd done so it was to try to save someone's life. The second time, it was a complete accident. Okay, so probably best to avoid a third time even if my motivation was being a good friend.

Leaving the glass where it was, I returned to my search. I ventured lower to look under pieces of furniture. I surmised, since the glass broke when Agnes fainted, that the ring could have taken a slip-and-slide ride to a dark, remote corner of the room.

Seeing no other way around it, I dropped to my knees and started directing the light under the cabinets and furniture, praying a flash of green from the emeralds or white brilliance from the diamond would greet me and not the beady eyes of some multi-legged insect who'd taken refuge in the darkness. A shiver slithered down my spine at the thought of being practically eye to eye with one. But a girl's gotta do what a girl's gotta do.

So far, I'd come up empty, both on the diamond and insect prize—at least fifty percent of which I was grateful for. Only one piece of furniture left. I made sure I didn't crawl over the area where Rico's body had been. There had to be some kind of rule against that somewhere. Like stepping on a grave. Bad luck had to follow if you desecrated the dead—even if it wasn't official yet.

I leaned lower and shone the light one final time under the mahogany hutch. No beady eyes. No brilliant gems. But there was something. Holding my breath and hoping nothing crawled over my hand, I reached under and pulled out a plain manila envelope. Sealed and no name. I might not be able to find a pulse on a person, dead or alive, but the size, weight, and feel of this package indicated to me it was stuffed with cash.

Getting up off the floor, I stretched out the kinks and grabbed the largest piece of the glass, worried that someone might get hurt. The small shards were dangerous, but the jagged remains of the glass could be deadly if someone slipped and fell. I moved back into the kitchen, closing the door behind me. I set the glass on the counter for the police in case they needed it for whatever reason. Since I was positive Rico's death was an accident, all the rules drilled into me by Detective Pizza Guy shouldn't apply, right?

The light from my phone caught the glass at just the right angle, and I noticed something reflecting on the inside. Closer inspection revealed silver and green flecks. In a flash, I was transported back to my high school days when my boyfriend had given me a beautiful ring. I'd been suitably impressed and had almost given him the gift that could only be given once until I'd decided to clean the ring before our big night.

Similar flakes had appeared in the glass housing both my ring and the jewelry cleaner. Turns out the cleaning solution had revealed the ugly truth about my boyfriend and his gift—they were both fake.

CHAPTER FIVE

———

Realizing the ring was a fake, my mind started the hundred-yard, dangerous dash to assumptions and conclusions. I didn't want to think the worst of my newest friend, Agnes. She'd been through a lot. She deserved happiness. Unfortunately, Rico didn't seem to be the one who was giving it to her. Agnes had mentioned—several times—about how challenging their brief, shared life together had been. Had Agnes noticed the ring was fake and decided to invoke the till-death-do-us-part segment of their vows? Though I never planned to get married, if I did, you better believe there'd be a clause in there that clarified that death had to come from natural causes and not a result of my spouse prematurely ending my life because I'd become too big of a pain in the asteroid to live with.

Then there was the worry about Agnes's increased drinking. Though we hadn't been close friends before the interview, she'd been to the tavern numerous times. She'd never consumed more than one drink during her visits—until this past week.

Regardless, my belief that the ring might be fake didn't prove that Agnes believed that or that she'd decided to take matters into her own hands. Add that to the fact that I couldn't find the ring and you ended up with me keeping my big mouth shut. Hey, a girl can learn, can't she? I did worry, though, that Agnes might be in more trouble than being down to her last bottle of tequila.

I needed to get back to the tavern but wanted someone to be here when the police arrived. *If* they ever arrived. Agnes used to work at the police station. You'd think they'd be more prompt when it was one of their own—even if it was a former employee.

I headed next door to the Stewart household. I knocked until Mrs. Stewart answered the door.

"Why hello, Lilly. What brings you to my back door?"

She was smiling, but I was certain she wondered who I thought I was to skip the traditional guest route to the front door and just make myself at home out back. "I'm sorry to bother you, but there's been an accident. Agnes is with Rico at the hospital, and the police should be here any minute. I really need to get back to the tavern. Do you think you could wait next door for the police?"

Mrs. Stewart's expression morphed from curious to serious. "Is Rico alright?"

Have I mentioned how much I hate being the bearer of bad news? For the official record, really hated it. I decided to soften the truth a bit. After all, I wasn't exactly sure what Rico's current status was. "He's receiving the best possible care. We can only hope for the best. Would you be willing to wait?"

She nodded. "Of course. Just let me grab my e-reader. I'm halfway through Elizabeth Ashby's last book. I can't seem to put it down."

I waited while she collected her things, and wished I had time to read a good book. Just like Clara and Tara, she was efficient and managed to be back in less than two minutes.

"Thanks so much. You may want to wait on the back porch. Agnes decided to create her own cleaning solution, and the result produced a rather strong odor."

Mrs. Stewart moved one of the chairs to sit close to the back door. "I should be able to hear the knock." She looked at her watch. "You probably need to get back to the tavern. Lunch rush will be starting soon."

"Thanks again."

I put the envelope of what I assumed to be cash in the basket of my bike and headed back to the tavern. During the ride there, I reviewed everything that had happened this morning to see if any cosmic interlocking puzzle piece jumped out at me and helped me put the picture of what happened together. I stopped about a quarter of a mile from the tavern and dialed the number for Agnes.

"Hi, Lilly. Did you find the ring?"

With a slow exhale, I offered the bad news. "I'm sorry. I couldn't find it."

"Oh…"

"How's Rico?" I felt like that information should have priority over a fake ring.

"They're still with him, but it doesn't look promising."

"I'm sorry."

"Me too."

I waited a couple of beats before sharing news of what I *did* find. "While I didn't find the ring, I did find something of interest under the hutch in the dining room."

"Oh?"

"I found a sealed envelope. I didn't open it, but if I had to guess, I'd say a stack of cash."

There was the distinct sound of sniffling. "I have all the money I could ever want or need. We both should get rid of our money, Lilly. It's cursed. My husband is most likely dead. I've felt sick almost since I got off the boat a couple weeks ago. I've managed to lose my ring, and all you've found is more cash. Keep it. Give it to charity. Do whatever you want with it. None of that matters now."

I wasn't comfortable doing any of those things with an envelope of cash. "I'll hold on to it for you and drop it off to you later. Will you keep me posted about Rico?"

"I will, but you and I both know he's gone. The medical personnel are doing their job, but I know it in my heart of hearts."

Agnes was right, but I felt compelled to not agree with her. "Call or text if you need anything. Try to get some rest while you're waiting. We'll deal with all of this later today or tomorrow." I wanted to tell her everything would be alright soon, but not even taffy-truth could be stretched that far.

I was about to end the call, when I heard muffled voices again. I waited. The moment I heard Agnes choke back a sob, I knew. My heart broke for my friend. Though they might not have been in love, I believed she cared about him.

"He's gone, Lilly. I'll have to catch up with you later. There are arrangements that must be made."

I blinked back a few errant tears myself. I didn't cry for many reasons, but death was at the top of the list. "Call if you need anything. Do you want me to see if Mrs. Stewart can come stay with you?"

"No. I want to be alone." The sound indicating the call had ended chimed in my ear. Guess there was nothing more to be said.

My remaining ride back to the tavern was slower than I'd planned. The weight of everything that had happened this morning added to the sluggish response of my muscles. Any remaining energy was diverted upward to my brain. I wanted to believe Rico's death was an accident. That was what the paramedic had believed. *Don't borrow trouble from tomorrow. Let today's be sufficient.* Gram's words of wisdom floated into my thoughts. She was right. No sense in suspecting foul play, especially not quarterbacked by a friend, until those in a more official capacity blew the whistle. The good Lord knew I had plenty to say grace over right now anyway.

The tavern was bustling when I arrived. I'd barely made it into the office to put my purse away when all the tavern personnel but Ruby crowded in at the door. I gave them the sixty-second version of what had happened. Though Rico was new in town, Agnes had been here for years and was part of the Danger Cove community family. I knew that within hours of the news spreading, people would be doing whatever they could to help Agnes get through this tough time. It was how small towns rolled and one of the reasons I loved it here. Once I'd shared, I needed one small piece of info in return from them about my newest (and currently tardy) employee and gardener. "Drake?"

"Out back," Freddie supplied.

I nodded. "Okay, thanks. I'm going to check in on Ruby and then head out back to speak with Drake. Thanks to all of you for taking care of business while I was away."

They nodded and returned to work. I slipped behind the bar and waited for Ruby to finish with a customer. Even though she didn't officially work at the tavern, she helped out from time to time whenever we were short staffed. With Hope out of the country, she'd been a real godsend lately. "Hey, Ruby, thanks for covering. I'll fill you in on all the details later, I promise. I need to check on Drake first, and then I'll take over. You can have some lunch before heading out—my treat."

Ruby laughed. "With both of us basically retired now, Vernon practically jumped at the chance to get me out of the house. We've had entirely too much quality time together. He swears I've been doing the *Lord of the Dance* yoga pose on his last nerve. When I offer meditation to help him relax, he says a scone or chocolate cake from the bakery would have the same effect."

I swear I wanted to be like them when I grew up. That was how I envisioned my life with Tanner. Well, maybe a little less fussing at each other. Happily cohabitating, enjoying each other's company, and avoiding the commitment coma. You know you've seen it. When couples are together for a long time, they sit at dinner and don't speak to each other. They fall into a routine that is safe and sleep inducing. "I bet Tara has some kind of sweet treat back there. She usually keeps some on hand in case I need to butter up Officer Faria."

Ruby put her hands on her lean hips. "I'm pretty sure you butter up my guy the same way when you're looking for information."

My cheeks heated. She was right. I did. Vernon had some pretty tight connections with all kinds of law enforcement. He'd told me he was a retired schoolteacher, but I wasn't sure that was the whole story. Either way, both he and Officer Faria had proven a valuable resource for information when I needed something checked out. You wouldn't think a bartender would need to have things "checked out" from a police perspective, but I'd found myself in a situation or two in the past that required just that. In exchange for information, I gave them their favorite sweets.

I shrugged and smiled. "A girl's gotta do what a girl's gotta do."

She waggled her finger at me. "Go. Check on your new gardener. Don't be too long. These old bones aren't used to this anymore."

Late spring in Danger Cove was the perfect time of year. The weather was moderate, flowers were blooming, and the tavern's gardener was working in the soil to produce the wonderful fruits and vegetables Clara and Tara used to serve up their amazing dishes. I confess seeing the garden come to life made me miss our old gardener, Abe, very much. Thanks to circumstances outside of his control, he'd had to move on from Smugglers'. I'd wished him all the best when he left, but really hated that he'd had to leave.

The new guy, Drake Butler, was tall with a muscular build, dark hair, and looked to be about a decade or so younger than Abe. There was an air of mystery surrounding him, but until his background check came back confirming something was wrong, he fit three very important criteria: willing, able, and available. That trifecta of talent had prompted me to hire him on a probationary basis.

"Hey, Lilly. Sorry about being late. I got tied up taking care of some business in town. You'd be amazed at how much there is to do when you first move."

Since I'd moved here a little over a year ago, I knew he was telling the truth. "I get that. Next time, call or text if you're going to be late so that we can plan ahead. Deal?"

He ran his fingers through his black waves of hair and offered a contrite grin. "Yeah, I hear ya. Again, sorry." He paused a moment. "How'd things go this morning? You had a brunch or something with that fancy-pants chef, didn't you?"

I started to ask how he knew, but chalked it up to small-town grapevine. More effective than social media when it came to sharing news. "It was eventful." Since I didn't want Drake to feel left out from the rest of the team, I quickly hit the highlights of the food served and the impromptu visit of Jonathan's ex. I wrapped it up with, "The ambulance arrived at Agnes's house, and she confirmed with a phone call on my way here that Rico didn't make it."

Despite the sun hanging out high overhead, a shadow of darkness descended on Drake's face when I shared the news.

I reached out and clasped his forearm gently. "I'm sorry. Did you know him?"

Several seconds of strained silence settled between us. "Sorry. I just hate to hear about something like that happening to anyone. Makes you feel bad for the family." After a beat, he brightened. "Do you have a few minutes? I'd like to show you a few things in the greenhouse. Maybe some beauty will help dispel some of the darkness from this day."

The way he had phrased his last sentence made him sound like a poet—which didn't fit his rough exterior. Maybe he was like Tara's meringues—hard on the outside and soft on the inside. I stifled a giggle. Tanner wouldn't like me comparing Drake to a sugary dessert. Wanting to stay professional, I reflected instead on how seriously Drake seemed to be affected by the news of Rico's death.

It didn't take a bachelor degree in bartending to know when someone didn't want to talk, so I'd try not to pester him about it. Besides, I needed to be inside to relieve Ruby as quickly as possible. "I can take a few minutes, sure. I'd love to see what you've got going on."

The moment I stepped inside the modified greenhouse, a melody of scents played to my nose. The idea for the greenhouse had been Abe's. He had built a wooden structure with two large rooms. The one farthest from the door doubled as his office and served as an additional place to store supplies. Both rooms offered temperature control for some of the flowers and plants. There was also an extension off those areas that utilized the glass customary in greenhouses, which amplified the warmth of the sun and allowed him to grow a variety of items, all used to make the dishes served at the tavern among some of the best in the area. I might be biased about that last part, but it was my story and I was stickin' to it.

"It smells great in here."

We walked past a variety of roses. The urge to touch and smell them pulled on my sentimental strings. Those were Gram's favorites. I noticed the thorns and decided to wait for a more leisurely visit rather than a walk-by touch. No sense in doing something that required the use of bandages for the rest of my shift. "You decided to grow some flowers too?"

Drake stopped in front of a flower I didn't recognize. He grinned as he ran his fingertips over the petals of a white flower colored in various shades of pink and red. The freckles dotting the surface reminded me of Agnes's complexion.

"I thought it would be nice to have fresh-cut flowers to go on the tables. This one is a Stargazer lily."

I smiled. Fresh flowers were a great idea. "It's beautiful."

He opened his mouth like he was going to say something, but then closed it again. "Let me show you the herb garden."

We moved to another area back in a corner. The moment I stepped closer, the fragrance of sage, rosemary, and thyme greeted me. "It smells like an Italian restaurant."

He grinned. "Tara mentioned wanting to explore Italy a bit with her dishes. I wanted her to have the freshest possible herbs to work with."

I thought of the possibility of Tara leaving to go work with Chef Jonathan and managed to swallow the sugar cube–sized lump of emotion forming in my throat. "That's very nice of you."

Wanting to divert my thoughts, I took in the palette of colors from the flowers, the vibrant green leaves of the plants and herbs, along with the way he'd arranged them in an aesthetically pleasing manner. I noticed a bottle of tequila sitting at the end of one of the shelves. I might not know a lot about horticulture, but I didn't think that was among the recommended sources of nutrition. "You're doing a great job. Now that the weather will permit planting outside, I'm looking forward to some fresh fruits and veggies from the garden as well." I pointed to the tequila bottle. "Though I'm pretty sure that doesn't belong here."

Drake shrugged and offered a quirk of his lip. "It is what you hired me to do, and…" He grabbed the bottle. "This was my reward for completing all my errands today. I promise it's going home with me tonight."

Seemed reasonable. Until I caught him drinking on the job, I'd trust that what he said was true. My gaze was drawn to a vibrant purple flower on the opposite side of the room. Moving toward it, I lifted my hand to reach out and touch what I knew would be the softest silk.

"Lilly, stop!" Drake's shout startled me, and my arm fell to my side absent of its prize. I turned, embarrassed and unsure why he'd yelled. I'd seen him touch the flowers earlier. Maybe he was possessive, even though all of this technically belonged to Hope.

"What's wrong?"

He moved between me and the purple petalled plant. "This flower is monkshood. Very dangerous. Even a touch can cause unpleasant effects."

Like the EMTs, I lacked the ability to possess a poker face. As a result, I was sure he could see my face twist into concern. "Why are you growing it here then? I know not too many people come in here, but still. We certainly can't put them out on the tables."

He shot me a sheepish grin again. I was betting earlier in his life that got him out of trouble more times than he could count. At some point though, the facial expressions would stop working. Pretty sure Drake had hit that point today.

"It's such a beautiful flower. I couldn't help myself," he explained. "How about if I post a warning sign or move it back into my little office area?"

I was such a softie. "Both are necessary if you want to keep it around. I don't want to have to explain an accidental poisoning to Hope."

He grinned and slipped on a pair of gloves before carefully picking up the flower. "You got it. Moving it now and a sign will be up soon."

My phone buzzed in my pocket. A quick glance confirmed it was Mandi indicating the lunch rush was in full swing. "I have to run. Thanks for the tour."

"Anytime."

I was tempted to remind him once again about a few of the items we'd talked about: Don't be late. No drinking on the job. No poisonous plants without appropriate warning. But, really, should a person need to be reminded twice about such things? I was going to go with no.

Drake followed me inside. "You want me to help out in the kitchen?"

Clara and Tara were bustling around preparing food for the incoming orders. "Check with Tara. I'm sure she'd appreciate the help."

The drama and trauma of the morning set aside, it was time to focus on the tavern. From the number of patrons currently seated at the bar and in the dining area, there would be plenty of distractions to keep my mind occupied.

A couple hours later, the rush was finally over. I made my way to the kitchen to grab a cup of tea when my favorite detective—not—Marshall was waiting for me. His crossed beefsteak arms coupled with the red hue of irritation on his face sent a clear signal that not even a deluxe, extra-large pizza from Gino's Pizzeria would pacify him. Thankfully, Officer Faria was hanging out behind Marshall's bulky form. "Afternoon, detective. What can I help you with?"

He jerked his head toward the kitchen. "In private, please."

Shitzu, this could not be good. I forced a smile. "Sure, come on back. Ruby, would you mind covering again for a few before you head home?"

She patted my arm. "Sure thing. Call if you need anything."

I nodded but didn't say anything. Truthfully, it was taking all my energy to keep my facial expressions neutral and avoid anything that might irritate Danger Cove's finest this afternoon. Once in Hope's office, Detective Marshall handed me a piece of paper. "This is a search warrant."

My fingers trembled a bit as I unfolded the paper and skimmed over the contents. I didn't understand all the legal jargon, but the gist of it was they had the right to search the entire premises of Smugglers' Tavern *and* my residence. I shook my head as I handed it back to him. "I don't understand. Should I call my attorney? What are you looking for? Did something happen while I was gone?" I looked to Freddie and Drake, both of whom were lurking outside the door, pretending not to be eavesdropping. "Other than the fifteen minutes I was in the greenhouse with Drake, I've been at the bar for the lunch rush." At least this time I was on the asking end of the twenty questions game.

The detective put his hands on the desk and leaned forward, dangerously close to invading my personal space. "Mrs. Iglesias filed a stolen-property report a little while ago. The initial investigation at the scene revealed *your* fingerprints all over the place. Most incriminating evidence is you leaving your mark on the glass where the ring was being cleaned."

His small smile of satisfaction sent a shot of surly straight to the tip of my tongue. "Would you like to hear my side of the story or just arrest me now so you can get back to the pepperoni pizza I know is waiting for you?"

Admittedly, that might be more like a pound of surly rather than a shot, but my history with this particular dispenser of justice did not bode well for him actually hearing me out. I decided to go ahead and try to share my version of events before attorneys had to be called in. "I was at the house. Agnes called me, distraught about Rico. I was the one who called 9-1-1. My prints were on the glass because…"

Detective Marshall held up his hand to stop me. "My men are on the clock, Ms. Waters. We have a search warrant and intend to execute it. Save the sob story for your attorney." He turned to Officer Faria. "Get the team. Start out back. Search everything." He returned his attention to me. "We'll do our best to be done before the dinner rush."

At least he gave me that. I wasn't sure why, but I'd learned enough to know now was the time to be grateful. "Thank you. I appreciate that."

He nodded. "Go on about your business. We'll let you know when we find something."

I managed to harness my tongue before it shot off another snarky comment. He wasn't going to find anything. I didn't steal the ring—I couldn't even find it when I'd been looking for it. I also had every intention of returning the envelope of cash I'd found while cleaning. Honest Abe had nothing on me. Once the men in blue had moved outside, I returned to the bar. I needed to keep busy so that I wouldn't call or, better yet, storm over to Agnes's house to demand why she hadn't explained my presence to the police.

Once Ruby had been filled in, she headed to the kitchen for a break and to wrangle up some food and dessert for Vernon. Thankfully, the crowd at the bar was occupied with friends, so I didn't have to chat any of them up too much. I kept replaying the scene at Agnes's house over in my mind. Had this all been some elaborate setup? She'd been unhappy with Rico—there'd been no secret about that. Was discovering the ring was a fake the last straw? No matter how much I reviewed my history with her though, I couldn't come up with why she'd have it out for me. Not because I was perfect. Goodness knows that wasn't the case. And despite what Detective Marshall thought, I'd taken extra care to not disturb the scene this time. Agnes had to play my heartstrings to even make me go near it. Other than moving the large piece of the glass to the counter and holding on to the envelope of cash I'd found under the cabinet, I hadn't really done anything at all.

"Lilly?"

Officer Faria broke into my thoughts. "Are you done?" I fought to keep the irritation out of my voice, but wasn't sure I succeeded.

"I'm going to check in here and in the restroom area. Just me and one other plainclothes man. We'll try to be as unobtrusive as possible."

"Where's Marshall?" That time there was no doubt irritation laced my words.

"He's just doing his job. We have to follow up on all leads in an investigation."

"Does that mean not allowing me to explain?"

Faria shrugged. "The way he said it wasn't right, but what he said was. Once he is given a search warrant to execute, it's his job to do it. *If* he finds something that implicates you, then would be the time to take your statement."

I really hated when they were right and I was wrong. At least it was Faria pointing it out nicely rather than Detective Marshall lecturing me. Yeah, been there, done that. "You make a valid point." I wanted to explain to him why I was upset about Agnes, but decided to hold off. More research into that angle needed to be done before I spoke about it aloud to anyone else. "How is Agnes doing?"

He moved in closer, so I leaned forward under the pretense of wiping the bar down in front of him. "Mr. Iglesias' death has preliminarily been ruled an accident. Given her wealth and the possible stolen property, the coroner has decided to do an autopsy first thing tomorrow morning to rule out any foul play."

I nodded. "Thanks for sharing that with me. I know you didn't have to."

He smiled. "Consider it a peace offering. Now I better wrap this search up." His stomach growled, and he blushed.

"Should I ask Tara and Clara to make you something and put it in a to-go bag for when you're finished?"

"That'll be great. Thanks, Lilly."

He went about his work, and I put in an order for his favorite meal along with a few of the chocolate chip cookies we kept on hand for when he came in. Might as well pay it forward with the hopes he'd share the results of the autopsy. To avoid any appearance of impropriety, he would pay for his meal, but dessert would be my thanks to him for keeping us safe.

About fifteen minutes later, the door from the kitchen swung open, revealing Marshall's bulky frame. "Ms. Waters, your presence is required in your office."

I started to point out that it was Hope's office, not mine, but Mandi clearing her throat, accompanied by a smile and subtle shake of her head, sent the message loud and clear: *Play nice.* So I smiled and nodded. "Be right there."

Once he disappeared from the doorframe, I turned to Mandi, who was refilling some sodas at the bar, and stuck my tongue out at her. She just laughed. I managed to get my mirth under control before stepping into Hope's office. I decided it was time to take back control of this day. No better way to do that than restoring the norm, which meant going on the offensive with Detective Marshall. "Are you going to arrest me?"

His chest ballooned out as he took a deep breath. I was sure it was to keep from ripping me to shreds with his bare hands. Have I mentioned how big his hands were? "Not yet, Ms. Waters. However, our questioning of your staff revealed you were late arriving this morning."

"Which means?" Someday I'd try to buy a road map to this guy's mind so that I could understand all the twists and turns he took to get to the final destination of his point.

"Which means you had plenty of time to stop off at your residence to hide the stolen property before arriving here."

Unbelievable. I reached into my purse and tossed him my key. "Here. Knock yourself out. You aren't going to find anything because, like I keep telling you, I didn't do it."

He caught the key, which annoyed me, as I have butter fingers whenever someone pitches things in my direction.

"Nice try, but you'll need to come with me. We're not going to enter your premises without you there."

I was pretty sure they did that kind of thing on the police shows I watched, but maybe that was just television rather than real life. "I can't leave."

"You don't have a choice." His frame filled the room, and authority poured out of him faster than tequila flowed into Agnes's glass.

"I'll go and watch the search." Ruby's tone left little room for discussion. She entered the office, patted Detective Marshall on the arm, and offered a serene smile. "Okay?"

He paused for a moment and looked from me to her before nodding. "Okay."

Detective Marshall turned to leave the office. "Meet you outside in five, Ruby." He shot me one last warning look across the bow of the SS *Grudge Ship* he held against me for some reason. "As soon as I have proof, I'll be back to arrest you, and then you can tell me the story you keep interrupting me to share."

Once he left, Ruby smiled. "Don't let him get under your skin. He wants to get a rise out of you. It's a game to him." She nudged me with her shoulder. "I think deep down he likes you."

Her statement sent me into a fit of laughter. "If that's how he shows he likes someone, I feel sorry for whoever he chooses to love."

Ruby chuckled. "You may have a point." She grabbed her purse and the food containers. "Trust the universe, Lilly. Everything happens for a reason."

I sat down and thought about everything that had happened this morning. I decided the first thing I needed to do was call Agnes to determine why she hadn't explained to the police that my prints had only been left all over the scene because I was trying to help her. Did she really think I could've stolen her ring? Regardless, her actions—or lack thereof—had put me directly in Detective Marshall's line of fire.

CHAPTER SIX

The phone rang several times as I waited for Agnes to answer. It made me wonder if she'd found another bottle of her tequila and had drank till she discovered the nonexistent worm that used to be at the bottom. "Agnes, it's Lilly. Are you alright?"

"No, dear sweet girl. I fear I'm not. I'm in the hospital." The frailness in her voice rocketed me into a full-on guilt trip. All aboard—full steam ahead.

I wouldn't think making arrangements, paperwork, and whatever else one had to do when someone died at a hospital would take this long. "Still handling arrangements, or is something else wrong? Did you start coughing again from the fumes?"

"No. Remember I mentioned I'd not been feeling well since I had gotten back from the cruise?"

I did but had chalked that up to the increased tequila intake. "Yes, I remember." I couldn't find a way to delicately ask about the alcohol consumption, so I opted to be patient and see if she would volunteer any information. "Maybe you're just upset about everything that happened? I know you weren't happy with Rico. Sometimes guilt over unresolved issues can make us feel ill." *Like failing to mention to the police about my helping you this morning.*

"The relationship between Rico and I was complicated. Maybe I loved the idea of being married more than I loved him."

Other than the love I felt for my family, I wasn't sure I understood love enough to comment on her statement. I opted for neutrality. "Only you can decide that, Agnes. I'm sure, regardless of how you felt or didn't feel, you didn't want him dead." At least I hoped she hadn't.

There was a lot of silence on the other end—enough to make me wonder if maybe she *had* harbored homicidal thoughts, especially after discovering the ring was a fake. I was just about ready to say something, when I heard retching and the sound of someone losing the contents of their stomach. I put my hand over my mouth to prevent the same thing from happening to me. It was true. I was a sympathy puker. Even if an animal made the sound, it sent me straight to the bathroom.

I was about to disconnect the line when a woman came on. "Hello?"

"Yes?" I swallowed hard, closed my eyes, and pictured the sun setting over the water to help calm the roiling in my stomach.

"This is Nurse Williams. Mrs. Iglesias is rather indisposed at the moment. You'll have to call back later."

Gladly! "No problem. Please tell Agnes that Lilly will try to stop by soon. I hope she feels better."

The call disconnected without any further comment from the nurse. I was sure she had more important matters to attend to than proper phone etiquette. Truthfully, I was thankful she'd hung up before I heard Agnes again. I felt guilty I'd assumed the worst about her, but a small part of me wondered how she would have responded to my comment if she hadn't turned ill. The cynic in me considered that maybe she'd taken the silence between us as an opportunity to make herself sick so she didn't have to comment about whether or not she'd contemplated what her life would be like with Rico out of the picture.

Neither scenario sounded appealing on my already sensitive stomach. I'd deal with those thoughts later. Time to go back to work. Before I could even make it out of the office, the phone rang. "Hello?"

"Lilly, it's Chef Jonathan. I wanted to see if you've made any decisions."

Nothing like direct and to the point. Seriously, did they not teach phone etiquette and polite conversation anymore? "I've been incredibly busy today since I left your little brunch." I remembered the threats Rico had made to Jonathan in the kitchen. "In case you haven't heard, Rico Iglesias was found dead earlier today."

"I'm sorry to hear that."

For the official record, he didn't sound sorry at all. "I'm sure you are. At any rate, both Agnes and I will need time to process everything. She's dealing with a lot right now, so please don't bother her."

He harrumphed. The sound caused me to smile a bit at his aggravation. Wasn't there a saying about misery loving company? Well, Agnes and I didn't want to be alone in our misery today. Granted, Agnes's misery ranked far higher than mine, but since I couldn't completely understand her role in all of this just yet, I couldn't give her all the sympathy I would normally extend.

"I understand it's been a difficult day for her. Life does go on, however, and I'm in a bit of a crunch myself. I'll give her a little time, but then I have no choice but to reach out to her."

Good thing for him I was a pacifist, or else I might want to crunch something more than his time. "Nice to know you put concern for others ahead of your own agenda."

"Lilly…"

"Have a nice day, chef. Good-bye." I hung up the phone, pleased I'd managed to maintain a level decorum with him that I currently didn't feel. I heard the bar calling. It was a safe zone for me. I could concentrate on work, have fun with my coworkers and the patrons, and forget about time crunches, hidden agendas, and stolen rings.

Tanner met me at the door between the kitchen and the dining room. "Hey, Lilly. I was just coming to get you. I've been covering at the bar, but there are some requests for drinks I don't know how to make."

I squeezed his hand. "Thanks for covering. I'll get right to it. I got delayed with a couple of phone calls."

"No problem." He reached into his back pocket and pulled out a newspaper. He held it up for my inspection. The black and white page on display had a few red circles on it. "I found some houses for sale that I think you might like."

Ugh, I didn't need this right now. "Tanner…"

"I know you have a lot going on, but life doesn't stop." He took my other hand in his.

The earnest look on his face sent the rolling rocks in my stomach into a full-blown downhill slide.

"I'm graduating. Your lease is expiring in about a month. It's time we look at what the next chapter in our lives together will be."

Was he really doing this here? Now? There was still plenty of time. I'd been a good tenant and was confident my landlord would work with me on a shorter-term lease if needed. And I had customers waiting. I exhaled slowly and offered the best smile I could dredge up from the landslide of my emotions. "I promise to look at this soon. Right now, I have to go. Customers waiting, remember?" I squeezed his hand and then extracted mine from his, bringing the paper with me. I held it up. "Thank you."

I made my exit before he could say anything more or the sad look on his face could drain what was left of my PLH—that's peace, love, and happiness—balance. It was dangerously low.

As I waited on my customers, my emotions located a pogo stick and started bouncing around all over my brain. Why was it every time you found a place of contentment in your life, circumstances tossed a big heap of time crunches and life-altering decisions into the mix?

"Want to talk about it?" Mandi brought some drink orders up to the bar.

"This is more of a discussion we should have over a pint of rocky road or other sinfully sugared sweets."

"That bad, eh?"

I nodded. "That bad."

"Tanner?"

You had to love the BFF wavelength connection. "He's part of it."

"You know he loves you, right?"

I knew…at least from what I understood of love. The women in my family had given their everything to the men they chose to love, causing them, in my opinion, to lose themselves. Though some found that very romantic, it was not a goal I had for myself. I'd steadily avoided that kind of commitment. I wasn't ready for an all-in type of relationship, not yet.

I put the drink tray in front of her and leaned closer so that she could hear my whisper. "That's what terrifies me."

The understanding and compassionate expression on her face transformed to disappointment right before my eyes. I might have forgotten for a moment that she and Tanner had known each other for forever and were like brother and sister. "You could do a lot worse, you know."

I would've preferred she had trounced me with some trivia about love or relationships. "As lame and cliché as this sounds, it's not him—it's me."

I could tell she was measuring her words carefully before she spoke by the way she closed her eyes, drew in a deep breath, and then exhaled completely before looking at me again. "I know you have some baggage from your mom and gram when it comes to falling in love..."

"More like an entire closet full." It was true, no sense in denying it.

"No one ever said love was easy, but you need to figure out how to open yourself to the potential for happiness."

Mandi picked up the tray and left me alone with my thoughts. Opening yourself to love could lead to happiness. It could also lead to heartbreak. Both were distinct possibilities from what I'd witnessed of love in my lifetime.

The rest of the day passed by without further incident, a fact for which I was eternally grateful. This might have been the longest day in recorded history. Okay, that statement bordered on the dramatic, but it fit my mood. Tanner had been pleasant, but I could tell he wasn't his usual cheerful self. I'm certain my lack of further comment on the house hunting hadn't helped his mood. Sunday night was usually a good time for us to have quality alone time, but since he was about to graduate, we'd decided to have an early celebration with Mandi and Freddie at the pier. Ice cream served as the perfect celebratory dish and a way to soothe over the sore spots of the day. Right?

With Monday being our only day off, we had to make the most of the one night we could stay up late without fear of the alarm clock the next morning. I arrived at the pier ahead of everyone else. They must've stopped by their homes first. As I had no food, no clean casual clothes, and no one to say hello to there, I didn't see much point in making that pit stop. Besides, a hot fudge sundae was calling my name. I heard it the moment I locked up the last door at the tavern.

I found a table toward the end of the pier, away from what remained of the tourist traffic. A blonde woman staring out into the dark water caught my attention. I couldn't be sure, but thought it might be Allyson Seavers. Maybe she'd tried Jonathan again and been rejected. See, perfect example of how love could lead to heartbreak. The shape of the bottle in her hand looked vaguely familiar, but I couldn't be sure of the brand or her spirit of choice since she was hanging out in the shadows just outside the glow of the lights. Regardless, I'd say love had not just turned its back on her. It was pushing her down a dangerous path.

Alcohol had never been my escape of choice, maybe because I'd worked in a bar for most of my career and witnessed firsthand the problems it could cause. Sugar, on the other hand, now that was a vice I could sink my taste buds into. Calorie consumption could make my problems seem less important, at least for a short time. Never mind the way those little buggers tried to hang out on my thighs long after the pity party had ended.

My first bite of cool vanilla ice cream surrounded by hot fudge sat on my tongue long enough to dispense soothing endorphins to my troubled brain. Yes, this was just what I needed to finish the day. I'd managed about five bites of happiness when Tanner arrived. His black jeans, white T-shirt, and black denim jacket suited him well. If he'd had dark hair, he could've doubled as James Dean. Gram used to tell me how all the girls would swoon over him. She'd even forced me to look at pictures of him on Google images. After taking in a tall drink of Tan, I'd take him over a dark-haired man any day.

Wanting to test the waters, I lifted my ice cream and smiled. "Wanna bite? I managed to save you a little."

"You never share your ice cream." He sat down at one of the picnic tables and gestured for me to do the same. It didn't take being his pseudo girlfriend to know his smile didn't reach those beautiful baby blue eyes of his.

I shrugged and pushed the container toward him. "A girl can change her ways sometimes."

"Are you going to change your mind about being in a serious relationship with me?"

And with one question, my ice cream comfort vanished. "Why the big push all the sudden? I've been honest with you since the beginning about my feelings on relationships." I moved the ice cream aside and took his hands in mine. "We have a good thing, don't we?"

"We do have a good thing. I want us to make it a great thing. Don't you want to be part of something great?"

I blinked hard to keep the moisture moving to the corner of my eyes from taking a joyride down my cheeks. "I already am."

He was silent for several painful seconds. "I've received an offer for a teaching job in Chicago."

Wait. What? "Why would you even apply to someplace so far away?"

He stood abruptly, pulling his hands out of mine. For at least an eternity and a half, which equals about two and a half minutes when you're waiting for what you know deep in your gut is a potentially life-altering explanation, he stared out into the fathomless depths of the dark ocean. Finally, he turned around. "Jenna is going away to college this fall. Mom has been dating some guy she works with and seems happy. Everyone is moving on to the next chapter in their lives. I want to do that too. With you."

It had been a long day, and I was tired. I tried pondering the movement math he mentioned, but it wasn't adding up. "And you thought you'd accomplish that by moving to Chicago?"

"You're not listening to me."

"I'm listening. I'm just not understanding. Why don't you dumb it down for the non-college blonde?" As soon as the words left my mouth, I wished for them back. At least that last statement. I tried for an immediate retraction of my word vomit. "I'm sorry. That didn't come out the way I wanted."

His strong jaw was set, and I could see him fighting to keep control of his emotions. Guess one of us should try.

"I should probably leave now. This conversation isn't going the way I'd hoped or wanted. Before I go though, let me try to explain the simplest way I know how. I love you. I want to take the next step with you. If you don't love me or are too afraid to take a chance on us, then maybe I should take the job in Chicago. I applied because it was a good opportunity at an amazing school, and I wanted to see if they would even take someone like me."

Sweet heaven, I'd messed this up royally. "Tanner, I'm sorry. I…"

He leaned forward and kissed me on the forehead. That was never a good sign.

"Please say you'll think about it, about us."

"Tanner, wait!"

He stopped walking away and turned around, but it was only long enough for him to get the final word in. "You know what the crazy part is? It's not like I asked you to marry me. I just thought we could find a place to move in together or, if you weren't quite ready for that step, at least having you invest in a more permanent home here in Danger Cove. It's important to me to know that you want to settle down here too. You're too afraid of commitment of any kind apparently."

He was right. Commitment did scare me. My mother's commitment to my father was strong. Strong enough to make her leave me with Gram when I was just a baby and follow him around for decades even though they'd never married. Gram's commitment to my grandfather was so strong that when he went missing in Vietnam and never came home, she could never move on to love another. I wanted to say something, but the words kept slipping on the hot fudge I'd consumed and couldn't make it out of my mouth.

Tanner walked back and pulled me into a hug. "Just think about it."

With those words, he was gone.

CHAPTER SEVEN

_____

Sleep was not my friend on the one day I didn't have to get up to an alarm. Thoughts of Tanner possibly leaving, Hope returning soon, Jonathan pressing, and Agnes...honestly, I had no idea what she was doing...filled my dream cycle with nightmares. The knot in my stomach would do any of the fishermen in the area proud, as it was tied so tightly, nothing was escaping. Wanting to feel at least slightly proactive, I picked up my phone and dialed the police station. When the operator answered, I forced a smile so that my tone would sound pleasant. "May I speak with Officer Faria, please?"

"May I ask who's calling?"

"Lilly Waters."

"One moment, please."

I'd yet to meet the woman who had replaced Agnes at the police station. Thankfully, Detective Marshall must have not poisoned her with regard to me yet, as she didn't take any tone or put me through the third degree. I liked her already.

"Morning, Lilly. You're up early for a Monday."

I forced a chuckle. "Don't remind me. Too much going on in my brain to sleep."

"Is there something I can help with?"

You couldn't get to yes if you didn't ask, right? So I decided to ask for exactly what I wanted. Besides, I was too tired to play games or employ some crafty strategy this morning. "Possibly. I was wondering if the autopsy on Rico had been completed yet?"

"No, not yet. Later today maybe."

It was worth a shot. "Okay, thanks. I'm sorry to have bothered you."

"No bother." He lowered his voice to a much quieter tone. "I do have some interesting news for you. Can you meet me at Cinnamon Sugar Bakery?"

Coffee, sweets, and information. Heck yeah, I could meet him. I tampered down my enthusiasm to a more appropriate level. "Of course. What time?"

"Will an hour give you enough time?"

"That will be perfect. See you there."

I noticed the police car already in the parking lot of the bakery when I rode up fifty minutes later. Once inside, I located Faria and waved to the owner, Maura. From what I'd learned through the town grapevine, everyone had been very excited when she showed up in town to visit and ended up not only helping solve a murder, but buying and reopening the bakery. Officer Faria, one of her most loyal customers, had referred to it as "the end of the dark times."

"You want your usual, Lilly?"

"That will be great. I'll be joining Officer Faria. Could you also put some of his favorite chocolate chip cookies on my tab?" I had no idea what the news was he wanted to share, but good or not, I wanted to be appreciative. Figured that was a good practice to keep up, especially with as much trouble as I attracted.

I slid onto the chair opposite him at a table next to the window. The shimmering walls reflected the morning sun and engendered a sense of calm. Well, either it was the paint or the smell of coffee and pastries. Regardless, it calmed my frantic mind a bit.

"Thanks for meeting me."

"Of course. Thank you for being willing to share."

He shrugged. "I can't share everything, but figure if I help you, you'll help me with information you run across. That's how it's supposed to work, right?"

"Right." I did feel good about tips I'd shared with him in the past that had helped to lead to some arrests. "What do you have for me today? I don't have any good info right now, but I've asked Maura to put together some cookies for you for later today."

He blushed. He may not enjoy sweets as much as others, but he definitely had a weakness for chocolate chip cookies. If he or his metabolism ever slowed down, those carbs were going to catch him and bury him in pounds. In the ultimate unfairness of gender inequality though, that tended to happen much later to men than it did women.

He leaned forward and glanced from side to side. "The ring was fake."

Time for me to win an Academy Award for my performance. I donned my best shocked face and replied in a loud whisper, "No way!"

He nodded. "Yes way."

"How did Agnes take it?" Now this I really wanted to know.

Faria leaned in. "I'm not sure, but she's the one who told us. Detective Marshall got the call, so the circumstances are unclear. She still wants us to find it though."

"Interesting." Time to offer a little quid pro quo. "I'm supposed to go see Agnes today to check in on her. If I learn anything, I'll let you know."

"Thanks, Lilly." He took another bite of a cinnamon scone and sipped his coffee.

I'd known him long enough to realize he was having an internal debate. About what though, I had no clue. I decided to practice the patience Ruby kept trying to teach me. God love her, she wouldn't give up, even though nine point nine times out of ten I failed miserably at it.

He finished off his coffee, and I wondered if my patience had been in vain. "Look, I can't say much, but part of our routine investigation turned up that Mr. Iglesias had some previous trouble with the law. Arrests, but no convictions."

"Arrests for what?" Hey, a girl could only be patient and quiet for so long.

"Can't say. I've probably said too much already. Keep this between us, okay?"

I didn't respond because I didn't want to lie to him. I wasn't going to blab it to Duncan Pickles or anything, but I was going to share enough with my other connection to the criminal justice system to see if he could find out anything more for me.

Thankfully, Maura walked up before I could answer. "Here's your to-go bag, officer. Compliments of Lilly."

He smiled. "Thanks, Maura." He stood and pushed in his chair before holding up the bag. "Thanks, Lilly. Talk to you later."

After he left, I flagged Maura down and placed another to-go order. This time it was for Ruby's significant other, Vernon. I wasn't sure how or from whom he got his information, but was grateful that he occasionally humored me with obtaining details I couldn't otherwise get. In exchange, I provided him with sweets that Ruby frowned upon. It was our own ends-justifies-the-means, unholy alliance.

I pulled out my phone to text Vernon with the information I needed and then paid my bill. I gulped down the rest of my tea, as caffeine would be critical for the long ride to the hospital. Thankfully, they hadn't taken her all the way to Seattle, or else I'd have to find an alternate form of transportation. Normally, I'd borrow Tan's car, but given the layers of ice forming between us, I didn't think that would be a well-received request. Besides, the long ride would tighten my calves and settle my nerves so I could come up with the best way to learn the most important detail of the day: Had Agnes killed her husband?

By the time I made it to the hospital, not only had I managed to develop enough heat in my legs to fry half a dozen eggs, but my brain had sufficiently scrambled the remaining half. Hopefully, I could wire enough of it back together to form coherent sentences.

With a few quick questions to the nice lady sitting behind the information desk, I made my way to the private room where Agnes was being kept. I slipped quietly into the room, not wanting to disturb her if she was sleeping. Okay, truth check. I wanted to see if she really was feeling as ill as she had sounded on the phone.

The room was dark, despite the early afternoon sun working valiantly to peek through the blinds. The hospital must use industrial-strength material in their window coverings. A pang of sympathy tugged on the sleeve of my blouse. I was used to a vibrant and vivacious Agnes. Instead of the vigor she usually tossed my way, her red curls lay flat against pale cheeks and caramel freckles faded into the hollows of her normally full cheeks.

"Agnes?" I whispered.

Her eyes fluttered open, and a small smile appeared. "Hi, Lilly. So nice of you to come."

The sweetness of her smile and the softness in her voice didn't sound like a woman capable of killing her husband and throwing one of her closest friends under the guilty bus even if she had known the ring was fake. Maybe I had this all wrong. I stepped a little closer and smiled. "Of course I came. I told you I would. How are you feeling?"

With no small amount of effort, Agnes managed to maneuver herself into a sitting position. She grabbed her stomach and exhaled slowly several times. "Still not well, though I haven't thrown up as much since I've been in the hospital. I miss my tea though."

"Don't they have tea here?"

Her eyes disappeared as she rolled them back into her head and waved dismissively with her hand. "You can't call that brown-colored water something as refined as tea. It's horrid, tepid, and undrinkable." Her tirade ended as quickly as it started as she sank back into the pillows. "Besides, the tea was a gift from Rico right after we got home from our trip. It makes me feel close to him."

It was times like these I wished, instead of an inner PLH barometer, I possessed a human lie detector. If the speaker laced their lies with some sugary words, I would inevitably fall into the sentimental sucker trap. Maybe I could get Officer Faria to teach me how to tell if someone was lying. I moved closer and took her hand. "I'll see if I can find you some decent tea and get it to you if you have to stay in here much longer."

One corner of her mouth quirked into a smile. "Don't suppose you'd smuggle some tequila in for me?"

I shook my head and chuckled. "Just because I work at Smugglers' Tavern doesn't mean I'm any good at smuggling. Besides, probably best to give your liver a bit of a break."

"You're right, of course. Plus, it helps me keep a clear head. I've been thinking…"

"About?"

"About who I might have seen lurking around the house when I came back from visiting Clara and Tara's parents."

This was interesting. Of course, I didn't know if she'd really seen someone or if, since I'd managed to roll out from under the guilty bus by not having possession of her stolen fake property, she was trying to find a new victim to serve as a speed bump. "Who did you see?"

She beckoned me closer. "That woman that crashed our brunch yesterday morning. The blonde…"

"Allyson Seavers?"

Agnes nodded. "I remembered the white blouse and dark jeans she had worn when she came into Charlie's restaurant."

"You think she had something to do with Rico's death?"

"I'm sure of it. She hated him and didn't have one nice word to say while she was there." She crossed her arms. "I know bad blood when I see it, and I'm telling you something happened in their past to cause it."

Though I didn't want to admit it, she had a point.

"Did Rico say anything about her when you got home?" Figured it couldn't hurt to ask. If she was lying, might as well make her keep spinning a solid story. She would either do just that or slip up and give me a thread to unravel her web of lies.

She closed her eyes, sending a few tears down her cheeks. If she was faking, I might have to relinquish my Academy Award to her for this performance.

"I asked him about her, but he pulled me into his strong arms and told me she was nothing but a blip on the radar of his past. I was his future."

There might be the tiniest bit of vomit in my mouth. I'd sensed from the beginning that Rico was a player when it came to the ladies. His handsome face, nice body, and Spanish accent slipping out phrases as sweet as honey ensured he didn't have to work hard to have women vying for his attention. My guess was Allyson had been more significant than Rico had let on. From the tension and hostility she fired his way yesterday morning, she was more like a minefield than a blip. "I don't doubt that. He didn't give her a second glance, but her reaction to his presence indicated that she thought they had some unfinished business. At least that's what it seemed like to me."

Agnes perked up at my statement. Great, not only was I no longer doubting her, I was helping her stitch together her potential quilt of lies. I bet Keely Fairchild, the expert quilt appraiser here in Danger Cove that Mandi had introduced me to recently, would have a field day with this.

"You're right, Lilly. If looks could kill, Rico would've been pushing up daisies."

At the familiar idiom, she stopped and covered her face with her hands. "Dear Lord in heaven, that's what he'll be doing now. Do you think she might have killed him?"

I didn't have a clue. It seemed risky for Allyson to come to the house on the off chance that Agnes had decided to visit her neighbors. And then she what? Stole the ring and killed him? There was no proof of murder...yet. Once I had confirmation he was killed and how, then I might be able to discern the truth from the lies. "I suppose anything's possible, Agnes. We don't even know the cause of death yet."

My words incited some dry heaves, and I decided it was time to take my leave. "I'll check on you later and bring the envelope of cash I found. I'm going to visit Bree and see if she has observed anything that might help us."

Agnes waved but kept her head over the plastic receptacle they'd left for her. Definitely not sticking around for any of that. I retrieved my bike and started the ride back to Danger Cove.

The Ocean View Bed & Breakfast was just down the road from the tavern. Bree was a regular at the tavern and shared the same knack as me for getting in the middle of sticky situations. Some people called it bad luck—we just called it life in Danger Cove. One thing became clear as I pushed my heart into a rhythm that would burn off all the calories I'd consumed that morning: Agnes might have appeared upset about Rico, but she'd never said the words aloud. It wasn't resounding proof of guilt, but I couldn't shake the feeling that it was something.

CHAPTER EIGHT

Bree was sitting in a rocking chair on the front porch when I rode into the area designated for parking. The afternoon sun highlighted her red hair. I couldn't see her eyes due to the sunglasses perched perfectly on her nose, but the relaxed position of her body along with the gentle rocking indicated she was enjoying some much-deserved rest. Not wanting to alarm her, I called out from my position at the bike. "Hi, Bree. Want some company?"

Her body became alert, and she waved me closer. "Hi, Lilly. You caught me taking my afternoon siesta. See what a vacation in Mexico will do to you?"

I occupied the rocking chair closest to her. "Vacation? Tell me more of this mythical fantasy of which you speak."

Bree chuckled. "You'd love it. There are beaches, waitstaff, and fantastic food."

I gestured to the sound of the waves crashing against the rocky cliffs nearby. "Hmmm, other than the waitstaff, I think I can find all of that here in Danger Cove. No passport required."

"Don't get me wrong—I love Danger Cove. It's just nice to get away."

I didn't want to burden her with more details of my life, including the fact it had taken me a long time to discover a new sense of home after Gram had died a few years ago. I'd made my way across the country, stopping for a time in places like New Orleans, Dallas, and Denver before arriving at Danger Cove. As a result, getting away was the last thing I wanted to do. "I suppose you're right. We missed you at the tavern while you were gone."

Bree stopped rocking and turned to face me. "I hear there's been no shortage of excitement surrounding you lately."

"I'd ask how you heard, but the grapevine around here works faster than high-speed broadband."

"Faster than what? Since when do you speak gigabytes and techno babble?"

"Since Freddie started taking an online computer class."

"Good for him. Make sure he doesn't learn how to tap into my Wi-Fi or cable service," Bree teased as she stood to pour us both a glass of lemonade from a pitcher on a nearby table.

"I'll do my best."

She handed me the beverage, and I downed the liquid like I'd been stranded in a desert for days. Guess the bike ride made me thirstier than I had realized. Once I drained the last drop, I placed the glass carefully on the acrylic table next to my chair. "Speaking of the drama surrounding me, you have any megabytes of data on some of your guests that might help fill the current vacuum of information I'm being sucked into?"

Bree laughed and poured me some more lemonade. "If you're referring to our notable guest, Chef Jonathan, I don't have much to share. He's been pretty quiet and keeps to himself."

"What about Allyson Seavers?"

"Other than the fact she's got it bad for the chef, what do you want to know?"

If she happened to have confessed to killing Rico, that would be nice information to have…Since I was sure Bree didn't have that information, as said grapevine had not revealed any police visits to the B&B, I'd have to settle for what I hoped was a much easier question. "After she left yesterday morning, what time did she return?"

Bree rocked back and forth a few minutes with her eyes closed, concentration settling over her rosy cheeks. "I can't be sure. Late morning maybe? I had to run some errands, and then Mom and Dad called. You know how they are."

I did. Whereas my parents had been absent from my life up until last Thanksgiving, hers were very involved and a little overprotective. "I think it's sweet that they call you almost every day."

"Sweet is one way to look at it. Don't get me wrong—I love that they care and check up on me, but once a week is more than sufficient. I was in my room yesterday with the curtains pulled and a cold compress on my head for the call," Bree teased. "When I came downstairs around ten or so, Allyson was sitting in the living room. For what it's worth, she was upset, and from the red circles rimming her eyes, I'm pretty sure she'd been crying."

If Bree's timing was right, then Allyson could have had time to show up at Rico and Agnes's house and do whatever she'd planned on doing and still have been back to Ocean View when Bree saw her—especially if the timing was more toward the "or so…" part of the time frame. "Makes sense. She had been pretty upset. Though I'd say it was leaning more to the angry side of upset rather than the emotional basket case side when I saw her yesterday morning around eight thirty."

Bree frowned, and her gaze narrowed. "Crying doesn't make you an emotional basket case, just human. I'm sure you've cried a time or twelve before."

I remembered crying a few times in the past ten or fifteen years—Gram's funeral offered up a veritable and repeated emptying of my tear ducts. I'd felt the emotions were justified under the circumstances. Crying wasn't something that had happened often in our house. Gram said tears only watered the dirt of life and muddied the problems you were trying to move through. She'd been a pillar of strength that never wavered in my life, no matter how much the winds of anxiety blew around her. But not everyone had a gram like mine, so I'd defer to Bree's assessment. "You're right. That doesn't mean anything other than she was experiencing some emotion."

My friend's red curly hair swayed with the tilting of her head as she studied me closely. I was sure she wanted to delve into a personal question or two, but I needed to get going. "If you think of anything else or learn anything new, you'll let me know, right?"

"Of course. What do you think she did?"

"I'm not sure, just that she had a serious issue with Rico, and now he's dead."

"I thought that was an accident."

"We're still waiting on the final results of the autopsy. And my centi-senses tell me something is going on here that doesn't smell right."

Bree laughed. "It still cracks me up that you say centi-senses rather than spidey senses. I thought you'd made peace with your parents and their band, The Barking Spiders."

"I did, but it's hard to change a lifetime of expressions in just a few months." Thanks to my parents abandoning me all those years ago to pursue a life with their weird band name, I'd developed an aversion to spiders and any reference to them. As a result, my intuition preferred to be called centi-senses rather than the more common spidey senses. Possibly a bit petty, but we all have our coping mechanisms.

"True that. Speaking of smelling, have you noticed how amazing Chef Jonathan smells?"

I shook my head as I stood. "Can't say that I've paid any attention."

"Bet you know what Tan smells like…"

As a matter of fact, I did—a breath of fresh ocean with just a hint of spice. Instead of answering her, I simply smiled and shrugged. "What does Jonathan smell like?"

"Like freshly chopped herbs. I'm not sure which ones since my thumb doesn't register anywhere on the green scale."

I could relate, as my thumb would be considered dried, brown, and crumbly—same as any plants I'd tried to tend to throughout my life. "I can ask Tara or Clara. Bet they know."

"That would be great. It's been driving me crazy."

"Short trip…" I couldn't help but tease her. She and I both had in and out privileges for Crazy Town. Most days we took the express train straight there.

Bree gave me a hug, grabbed the tray of lemonade, and headed inside with a final warning. "Try not to get caught up in the mess of Agnes's life. You have a lot on your plate between Hope coming back and Tan graduating. Focus on those things." She winked. "It'll be the best way to keep me from having to rescue you."

I started to grace her with one of my witty comebacks, when I saw Allyson returning from a walk. "Catch ya later, Bree."

"Later, Lilly."

Passing my bike, I walked directly toward Allyson on an intercept course. I had no idea what I was going to say or even if she would talk to me, but I had to give it a try. She wasn't really walking, more like gliding—a model taking her victory lap on *Project Runway* with her long, blonde hair lifting gently in the afternoon breeze.

Meanwhile, my hair continued to perfect its escape act from my ponytail and plastered itself to my cheek, thanks to the humidity and residual sweat from my long bike ride. Maybe she'd take pity on my disheveled self and provide information and a few beauty tips. I squared my shoulders and put on my friendliest face. "Hi. Allyson, right?"

Her brows knitted together as her gaze narrowed. "Do I know you?"

My ponytail swished from side to side as I shook my head. "No, not really. My name is Lilly Waters. I saw you briefly yesterday morning at Charlie's Cove."

The red in her cheeks deepened a few shades. "Oh…I'm sorry about crashing your brunch like that."

I waved off her apology. "You don't owe me anything. Truthfully, I didn't want to be there in the first place, so you weren't interrupting."

Her cheeks performed another kaleidoscope change of color, still red but less embarrassed, more of an angry hue. She crossed her arms. "Why did you go then? Don't you think Jonathan's been through enough already? Are you just leading him on about the possibility of investing in his restaurant?"

Umm, not sure where that sharp left turn came from. My innocent attempt to help her save face backfired and apparently sparked a whole box of fireworks in her brain. I lifted my hands in the widely accepted gesture of defense. "I'm sorry. No disrespect to the chef, just the timing of his request. I have my own restaurant and bar to run." Technically, not my own, but close enough for the purpose of this conversation. I decided to leave out the detail that he and Agnes had cornered me and refused to concede until I agreed to go to breakfast. She wouldn't be interested in that detail at all.

She turned and looked in the direction of the ocean. The wind still blew her hair directly behind her as though someone were holding a fan at the perfect angle. Seriously, how was that fair or even possible? "You're right. I'm super sensitive when it comes to him. I hurt him in the past, so now I'm trying to make up for that by trying to prevent anyone else from hurting him ever again."

Depending on what way I took that statement, it could lead me down a path ending in a nice, shiny motive for her killing Rico. If she'd learned that Rico had every intention of keeping Jonathan from Agnes's money, her protective instincts could have kicked in, and who knew what she was capable of then.

"I understand what you're saying, but matters of the heart are different than the business of a person's pocketbook."

My statement quirked the side of her mouth that I could see into a smile...or at least a half one. "Pocketbook? Does anyone call it that anymore?"

My turn to blush. I shrugged. "My gram called it that. Guess it stuck."

She nodded. "Nice way to remember her. She's passed away, right?"

"Yes. But how—"

"You referenced her in the past tense. Said she *called it* that rather than *calls*. I drew my assumption from there."

Beautiful and smart. I could see why Jonathan would be attracted to her. He was handsome in a way, but definitely dated up the social strata when it came to women like Allyson.

"You assumed correctly. We lost her almost four years ago now."

"I'm sorry."

Dampness gathered in my eyes—must be sweat or the salty sea breeze irritating them. I blinked rapidly to send it back into my maxed-out tear ducts. "Thank you. I loved her very much." I paused for a moment before continuing. "It's obvious to me that you love Jonathan. May I ask what happened?" I knew what Clara had told me the tabloids said, but I'd prefer to get it straight from the source. We'd see if she caught my use of the present tense when mentioning her affection for him. He might be over her, but she definitely wasn't over him.

She made no effort to stop the tears trailing down her porcelain cheeks. "Love makes us do strange things, Lilly. Sometimes what you have with someone is so perfect, you're certain it can't be true or last. Fear gnaws at you while waiting for something to destroy the happiness you've found. So instead of trusting in what you have together, you end up doing something that screws it all up." She turned to face me again. "I screwed up, and now I'm trying to make things right."

Guilt expanded in my throat, making it hard to breathe. She wasn't talking about me or my relationship with Tan, but her words hit home. I opened my mouth to try to speak to ask her how she had screwed up and, most importantly, if somehow it involved Rico. But before I could move enough of my vocal cords past the obstacle lump, a car pulled up, and Jonathan got out.

Allyson hastily wiped her cheeks, and a vibrant energy suddenly radiated from her. She waved. "Jonathan! Over here. Look who I found."

I wanted to correct her since, technically, I'd sought out and found her, but I was still trying to dissolve the emotions impeding my speech.

Jonathan took long strides until he was standing in front of both of us. "Lilly, so good to see you."

The feeling wasn't mutual, but now was not the time to be crabby. I'd prove I could play nice in the proverbial sandbox. "Nice to see you again so soon. Have you been enjoying our little town before you head back to the big city?"

He rubbed his hands together in excitement. "Actually, I was visiting Agnes."

This guy was unbelievable. "Seriously?"

Jonathan put his hands over his heart as if I'd wounded him with my words. Drama king. "I heard she wasn't feeling well. I feared it might have been something she ate, so I felt a responsibility to check on her."

"She's suffering from shock since her husband died yesterday morning within hours of eating your food." Admittedly, that might have been just a touch out of line, but this guy was not only standing on my last nerve, he was jumping up and down on it.

Allyson stepped in between Jonathan and me before I could continue giving him a small piece of my mind. "You know perfectly well that bastard didn't die from eating Jonathan's food."

I didn't *know* that, but was pretty sure it hadn't been brunch that had killed him, especially since we'd all eaten essentially the same food. I wasn't going to concede that to her though. "What did he die from then?"

"I...I mean...how am I supposed to know that?"

I shrugged. "You tell me. Since you have such confidence in what didn't kill him, doesn't that mean you must know what did?"

"Ladies, ladies. This is neither the time nor the place." He turned to Allyson and gently clasped her arms with his hands. "Despite the tragedy yesterday, this is going to be a good day."

He smiled one of those smiles I'd heard Mandi refer to as a "panty dropper." I did *not* ask where she'd learned that expression.

Allyson was soaking the smile up, and I'd bet my next paycheck that her panties were starting to slip. "You're right, Jonathan. Just being here with you again—in your arms—makes everything better."

He kissed her on the forehead before turning to me. "Agnes hasn't committed completely, but she indicated she was leaning toward investing in my restaurant. I hope you'll do the same."

The ocean breeze kicked up and wafted our way. Jonathan's scent joined it and carried to my nose a familiar scent—the Italian herb combination I'd experienced in the greenhouse with Drake. Both Jonathan and Allyson stared expectantly at me, waiting for some type of response. My problem with sharing my decline of his offer was that Rico had said no to Jonathan, and now he was dead.

I didn't want to make the same mistake.

CHAPTER NINE

—————

I arrived at my apartment at Hazlitt Heights about fifteen minutes after saying good-bye to Jonathan and Allyson. My farewell had to include a promise to give him an answer about both the investment and my coming to work for him. Of course, he wanted the answer in the next twenty-four hours or so.

My couch beckoned, but I opted instead for the beanbag chair that had stayed with me on my journey from New York to Seattle. It was the only piece of furniture—if one could call a beanbag chair furniture—that I'd brought with me every step of the way. As weird as it sounded, after Gram died, it was the one constant in my life. Okay, not weird…pathetic, but true.

The room disappeared behind my closed eyelids as I contemplated whether or not I should take Jonathan up on his offer. Funny how twenty-four hours could swing your position from one side to the other. With Hope returning and Tan possibly leaving, that left Mandi and Freddie. I adored them both, but how long until they got on with their lives? Both were taking online classes, so eventually the day would come when they would move on to bigger and better things. I didn't blame them. Not one bit. For me though, this *was* my bigger and better thing.

The big question was: without Tan, would it continue to feel the same? And I couldn't ignore the question niggling at the back of my brain. *If* Jonathan had killed Rico, then he probably wasn't someone I wanted to pull up roots for and follow to California. Never good to work for psychopathic killers, regardless of how harmless they seemed otherwise.

Allyson's words repeated in my head on an annoying audio loop. Was I intentionally sabotaging a good thing believing it was going to blow up in my face anyway? I didn't think so. I'd shied away from romantic notions of love and relationships long before I met Tanner. He was the first person I'd even allowed myself to venture into that territory with since the faker from high school. And now he wanted more. I flopped back into a reclined position on the beanbag to contemplate another decision I had to make soon. What to get Tan for graduation.

Things were rocky between us right now, no doubt, but I still wanted to get him something. He'd worked so hard. He deserved the recognition and to be rewarded for his efforts even if we couldn't reconcile our differences.

Fear gripped my heart in an icy vice. What if he was still upset and didn't want any kind of gift from me at all? Ugh, I hated feeling this way. Was it wrong to want everything to go back to the way it was before I even had the kind of money that would allow me to buy a house? If I were living paycheck to paycheck, my apartment would be the only option I could afford. Of course, that wouldn't negate the idea of Tan and me moving in together. Could I find a way to overcome my fear of commitment? Or, as Allyson had predicted, would I keep stomping on any happiness I might be able to find? Before I could continue my merry-go-round of self-incrimination and doubt, my cell phone dinged with an incoming email.

Grateful for the distraction, I glanced down at the small screen to see the message was from All About You Investigative Services. Corny name, but I'd heard good things about them, and their Angie's List segment gave them an A+ rating. Not wanting to read the results of Drake's background check on my phone, I managed to pull my sorry butt up from my sad-sack position and head to the bedroom where my laptop was set up.

A few minutes later, I was scanning the report. The vice grip around my heart released its hold long enough to aim lower before resuming a death grip, now on my stomach. Drake had an arrest on his record. My brain kicked in and sent a message to the claw around my stomach to ease up. Lots of people got arrested. Didn't mean they were guilty or had a conviction on their record. The tequila bottle in the greenhouse made me think it could've been something as simple as public intoxication.

Serious, but not as gut wrenching as a DUI, theft, or other termination-worthy offenses. Still, I needed to know what path of criminal negligence his arrest placed him on before I made a decision about whether he could remain in the employ of Smugglers' Tavern.

I considered replying to the investigator who'd completed the report that simply telling me someone was arrested, but not sharing the details of the transgression, didn't qualify as *all* about the person. I guess for twenty dollars how much could you really expect? I could ask Drake, but because my internal lie detector still needed fine-tuning, I decided to add to my Cinnamon Sugar Bakery tab instead and texted Vernon, asking him for details. I mean, he was already checking on Rico for me. What was one more, right? I might have to pull out a whole cake for this one, but it would be worth it. If Drake was a problem, I'd need to have him dealt with before Hope returned.

Vernon's reply that he'd looked into it was accompanied by an emoji with rolling eyes. My guess was he'd probably meant to send the little guy that represents being not amused, but as someone new to the emoji world, Vernon was still learning. Or…maybe he did mean to roll his eyes at me. Either way, I was happy for his help. I texted back a thank-you accompanied by lots of smiley and other funny faces. It was so high school, but if it made him chuckle, shake his head at me, and get me the information, I could live with that.

With that accomplished, I checked the time. Just a little after noon, and I was already exhausted. A nap might be the most productive use of my time. Sure there were things like grocery shopping, taking my bike in for a check, reviewing the paper Tan gave me for houses, and any other number of things normal people did on their day off. But, hey, I'd never claimed to be normal.

Instead, I crawled under the quilt my great-grandmother had made me and called my mom. After several rings, she answered in a groggy voice, "Baby? Is everything okay?"

Shitzu! I forgot for a moment that my mom wouldn't fall under the normal category either. Actually, she lived so far outside the norm for moms, it would take her a day by train to get there. "I'm sorry, Mom. Did I wake you?"

"Just dozing. We had a late show last night, and then there was some kind of problem with packing up the equipment. Personally, I think Brock needs to fire the roadies and get some new ones." She sounded a little more alert as she relayed what constituted a problem in her world.

"Isn't that something your new manager should take care of?" Since their former manager had been murdered after one of their shows last Thanksgiving, the band had been in a rebuild phase.

"I'm not sure how long *she* is going to work out."

I didn't even need to see my mother's face to realize the green-eyed jealousy monster had taken over. If the woman was a looker at all, I was sure she wouldn't last. My mother didn't mind sharing Brock with his legions of adoring fans as long as the stage separated them. But one-on-one as a member of the team, she wasn't going to stand for that. I chuckled at her response. "I can't believe you even allowed them to hire someone with double-X chromosomes or double Ds."

Harmony laughed at my comment. "I've missed you. How are you? How's Tanner? Am I going to be a gramma anytime soon?"

I closed my eyes against the onslaught of emotion her words prompted—some good, some bad. I wanted to be a mother…someday, but not any day soon. "Very unlikely."

"You know my grandmother biological clock is ticking."

"That's not a thing."

She laughed. "But it is to me."

"Does that mean you'll come visit more?" It was worth a shot, plus I was curious what her answer would be.

"Maybe. You know the band is going for a new sound, one you helped inspire, as I recall."

Her statement made me sit up straight. "What do you mean?"

"Remember the day you listened to Tommy and Johnny playing an unplugged set at Ocean View?"

I nodded even though she couldn't see. Though I didn't normally like the type of music the band played, I'd enjoyed that impromptu jam session. "I remember. It was a nice mellow sound with a great beat."

"Well, Johnny talked to Brock, and they decided to do an album that showcases their softer side. We sent you a demo. Did you get it?"

Moment of truth. I had received it, but not listened to it yet. "I hope to get to that today. I've been a little busy with everything at the tavern."

"Well, I hope you like it. There's even a song on there that he dedicated to you. Times are changing, Lilly. We may even find a permanent gig on the West Coast. We'll still tour a couple times a year because…well, that's in our blood. A consistent booking close to you, though, would be ideal."

It did sound ideal. I'd never lived close to my parents…ever. After the drop-off to Gram when I was only a few months old, I hadn't laid eyes on them until about nine months ago. The same nomadic roots that were alive in my parents lived in me as well. I think that was why I had trouble committing to a house. Apartments were temporary, houses much harder to pick up and leave. "I would like that very much."

"I'm sorry, baby. I have to go. I can hear Brock yelling, and it sounds like trouble is brewing. Can we talk later?"

"Sure, Mom. Give the old man a hug for me." I smiled thinking of the first time I'd called Brock that. He'd not been a big fan of the nickname, but tolerated it, as he knew I did it in fun.

"Will do. Love you."

"Love you too."

I disconnected the call, and even though I didn't get to talk to my mother about my problems, somehow I felt a little better after hearing her voice. I retrieved the CD they'd sent me and put it in the player before crawling under the quilt again. The first song was the one they'd named after me. I closed my eyes and let the soft beat, guitar strums, and bass line soothe some of the tension of the last twenty-four hours away. I recognized the djembe drum, as it was the same that Johnny had played that afternoon on the porch. As much as I hated to admit it, I really liked this new sound. And not just because I might have had a little something to do with it. I put the CD on repeat and fell asleep to the new sounds of The Barking Spiders.

The ringing of my phone woke me a couple hours later. Caller ID revealed it was Bree calling. "Hello?" It worried me that she was calling, especially since we'd just chatted recently. I also noticed a text from Mandi asking what I had going on this evening.

"What are you doing right now?" Her voice was so low that it made it hard for me to understand her in my sleep-induced haze.

"What? Sorry. I just woke up from a nap."

"Then you must be hungry."

"Umm, okay. Sure." I had no idea where she was going with this, but I'd learned to play along where she was concerned. There was generally a method to her madness.

"Why don't you casually stop by in about an hour. They should be headed out to Seattle by then."

"Who? What? Why?"

Bree laughed. "Do you always ask this many questions?"

"As a matter of fact, yes. I also want to ask if I can bring Mandi with me. She wanted to hang out this evening."

"Of course you can bring Mandi. As for your other questions, let me answer it this way. This has to do with something interesting I learned about Chef Jonathan."

"I don't understand. Why can't you just tell me?" Patience was not one of my greater virtues. To be honest, which was high on my virtue list, patience didn't even rank in the top ten.

"Because, my dear friend, this is something you need to taste to believe."

CHAPTER TEN

———

Bree wouldn't provide any further details, a fact I found very annoying. Thankfully, my nap had recharged my batteries, and I managed to keep my sarcasm and snark from coming out too much during my conversation with her. I texted Mandi to see if she wanted to join me. Her excitement about the Monday evening plans were expressed through multiple emojis…some I didn't even recognize.

We met downstairs by the bike rack. "I was afraid you wouldn't want to hang out with me," Mandi began as we unlocked our bikes.

I stopped my activity and looked at my best friend. "Why would you think that? I'm sorry I didn't reply to your text sooner. I was sleeping."

A curtain of red hair fell across her face as she lowered her head. "I might've been a little hard on you about Tanner yesterday evening."

Not wanting her to think I was upset at her for one second longer, I closed the distance between us and pulled her into a good old-fashioned hug. "Nonsense. You and Tan are friends, and you're looking out for him. I get that."

"But you're my friend too."

This was true. She was in a tough spot, caught between two stubborn best friends. Alright, one reasonable and one stubborn friend. No sense in denying the truth. I separated us so she could see the sincerity on my face as I sought to reassure her. "We'll figure this out. I would never make you choose between us or put you in the middle. Regardless of what happens between Tanner and me, we're all adults, and we're going to act like it."

Besides, if he moves and I leave, the entire situation will be irrelevant.

My words reassured her—glad that worked for one of us.

Mandi nodded. "We should get going. We don't want to keep Bree waiting." Her blue eyes sparkled. "I love that we're going on this adventure together."

We mounted our bikes and headed away from the apartment complex we both called home. I wasn't sure a bike ride to the Ocean View Bed & Breakfast qualified as an adventure, but either way I'd be spending the evening with my girlfriends and not thinking about Tanner, so that worked for me.

I pedaled hard—uphill, for the record—with Mandi matching me in speed and stamina. We made it there in pretty good time. The parking lot was empty, except for one car. Good, that meant there shouldn't be anyone around when Bree performed her big reveal. It had better be a very big reveal for all the cloak-and-dagger routine she was putting us through.

I knocked as we entered the front door. Not sure why since it wasn't a private home, but it still felt appropriate. "Bree? We're here."

"Come on back. I'm in the kitchen."

We made our way to the back of the house where there was a kitchen that looked like it belonged on the front page of one of those home décor magazines. Stainless-steel appliances, granite countertops, and white cabinets adorned the spacious room. The number of windows in the kitchen offered a bounty of natural light up until the sun set in the early evening. The fact that there was this amazing kitchen that rarely got used made me feel better about never using the appliances gathering dust in the same area in my apartment. Besides trouble finding us, that was another thing Bree and I had in common—our noticeable lack of culinary skills accompanied by a distinct lack of desire to follow in the footsteps of Betty Crocker or Martha Stewart.

Once inside the spacious room, I noticed the table was set for three. My stomach rumbled, reminding me lunch had been a long time ago. Wait. I think I slept through lunch. Breakfast was a very long time ago. "Did we have dinner plans?"

She brought out three plates from the oven and set them on the table. They looked like they'd been prepared by a gourmet chef. "Ummm, since when do you cook? Last I heard toaster pastries were your delicacy of choice."

Bree laughed. "Says the woman who only knows how to steep tea. At least Pop-Tarts have some nutritional value." She turned to Mandi, "Are you going to let her talk to me like that?"

Mandi giggled. "I've learned that ninety-nine percent of the time, you're perfectly capable of taking care of yourself."

Bree arched an eyebrow and smiled. "Ninety-nine percent?"

"Everybody needs a little help."

"I was only going to give myself a seventy-nine percent," Bree laughed.

I decided to join the conversation. "I could use some help filling my one hundred percent empty stomach. Can we eat now? I'd even be willing to use my one culinary skill to make us all a proper cup of tea after we've eaten. How's that for taking care of my friends?"

Bree shook her head. "You and Mandi are on your own there for tea. I prefer tea in the morning and coffee after a meal. Now please sit before all my hard work goes cold."

We did as she instructed. This was quite a surprise. Now at least I knew what she meant by something I'd have to taste. Once everyone was seated, I grabbed my fork and dove into whatever version of chicken was up as the main course. The flavors assaulted my taste buds—and not in a good way. More like someone had detonated a grenade of nasty in my mouth. My gaze darted around looking for a napkin, something, to dispose of this vile bite of whatever Bree had prepared.

I did a quick check of Mandi's reaction. Her eyes were wide as she chewed rapidly, I was sure in an effort to break down the dreadful food into pieces that would send the offending matter far, far away from her taste buds.

Mandi had always been more polite than me—no way was I going to swallow this…this…nastiness. My gaze resumed its search for something besides my hand, though a few seconds more and I'd resort to that.

After letting me suffer for several painful seconds, Bree lifted two paper towels in front of us. Mandi grabbed hers a scant second before I snatched mine. I sent the chicken on a return trip out of my mouth and then downed half the glass of lemonade she'd set out for me. Once I'd cleansed my mouth properly, or at least sufficiently until toothpaste and mouthwash could join the clean-up team, I met Bree's amused gaze.

"So did you like it?" Bree asked with a barely concealed smirk.

I was pretty sure spitting out food was a universal sign for *I'd rather starve than eat this again.* Even babies understood that simple gesture.

"It was an interesting combination of flavors. It's...uh...not exactly...well, not what I normally eat." I struggled to be honest and still be kind. Sometimes those two were in direct opposition of each other. "Maybe your tastes are more refined...Yes, that's it. My palate is not as refined as yours." Under the circumstances, it was the best I could do.

Bree's whole body was vibrating with her laughter now. I was glad she found this funny rather than being angry at me for not enjoying what she'd prepared.

"I didn't cook it."

That was a relief. "Thank goodness! Because if you had, I'd tell you not to quit your day job. Stick to breakfast catered in from Cinnamon Sugar Bakery."

"Lilly!"

Mandi's admonishment didn't dissuade me at all. We both knew I was speaking the truth.

I gestured to the remaining food on Mandi's plate. "You gonna finish that?"

Her adorable face scrunched up, smashing her freckles, and she shook her head. "Sorry, Bree."

"That's what I thought. So where did you get it from?" I knew it wasn't anything Clara or Tara had prepared. Even Charlie's cooking was miles better than this, so she hadn't had it catered in.

"They were leftovers from the meal Jonathan made for Allyson this evening before they left to visit Agnes on their way to Seattle for a date."

I could only hope my expression properly conveyed the level of bewilderment I currently felt. "They *ate* this garbage?"

"Jonathan savored it as though Emeril Lagasse himself had personally prepared the meal. Allyson was a little more reserved in her enthusiasm, but she smiled and finished the entire plate."

Maybe I'd just entered the Twilight Zone (not the kind with vampires that glittered in the sun—the kind where weird stuff happened to everyday people), but I couldn't fathom a universe where two people with refined palates could eat and enjoy this. "I don't understand. He's supposed to be *the* top chef, according to Tara."

Bree cleared the plates and fed the garbage disposal the remnants of our meal. That felt like a better fit than my taste buds and digestive tract. She popped a couple Pop-Tarts in the toaster and poured a glass of milk for each of us. "Dinner's on me tonight, unless you have plans with a certain hottie."

The thought of Tan and I *not* having a date tonight filled part of my empty stomach with despair. Normally, we'd hang out together every night we could. But I'd not heard from him since our argument yesterday. "Nope, no plans. What flavor are you serving up?"

"I believe in offering a variety to my guests, so you can pick two from the selection of chocolate fudge, apple pie, s'mores, or cinnamon sugar."

Now she was talking to my inner food critic. "You certainly know how to spoil a girl. As I know how much you like chocolate, I'll be happy to accept the apple pie and cinnamon sugar pastries."

"Excellent choice!" She turned to Mandi. "And for you, ma'am?"

"S'mores, always and only s'mores."

Bree made a big production of making our selections and then plating them. This time when she sat the food in front of me, I knew I'd enjoy every bite. A few minutes later, we'd finished off the first of our two tasty treats. "Five stars, my friend. You're top chef in my book." Thinking of Tara and her possible departure, I amended, "At least for tonight."

Bree refilled our milk glasses before turning serious. "Clara and Tara have nothing to fear from me. Though, I feel like I could give Chef Jonathan a run for his money if I gave it even half an effort. We have a world-famous chef here in Danger Cove that apparently can't cook. I'm open to theories."

Now that I'd pushed aside painful thoughts of Tan to a back room to deal with later and my tummy had been temporarily mollified, I focused on what I knew of Chef Jonathan. "The brunch he prepared for Agnes, me, and our guests yesterday was delicious."

"Did he make a chicken dish? Maybe poultry isn't his passion." She stopped, lost in thought for a moment. "Or, maybe the chicken I had in my fridge was nearing its expiration date—either is a possibility.

I thought back to the different meals served. "Yes, no chicken yesterday. There was a cinnamon raisin bread with custard and fresh berries and then eggs benedict with artichokes, I think. I'm not a fan of artichoke, but Agnes devoured it as though it were her last meal." I tried not to think about the fact that it *had been* Rico's.

Bree shrugged. "Then I've got nothing. Maybe he was just having an off day."

"That doesn't explain Allyson eating it without saying a word."

"I know they say love hurts, but this is ridiculous." That was the extent of my explanation at the moment.

"You don't cook very often, do you, Bree?" Mandi asked.

She had her thinking cap on. Hopefully, she could come up with something where we'd failed.

The corner of Bree's mouth quirked into a grin. "You could say that."

"Maybe the spices you have in your cabinet have lost their potency. I don't have the statistics on how long that normally takes, but I can find out if you believe it will be helpful."

Bree shrugged. "No need. It's not like I'm going to be using them anytime soon. I'll start replacing them slowly, as they can be very expensive. Not being Martha Stewart, would bland spices normally produce such a strong taste? I'm not disagreeing, just asking."

"Honestly, I don't know. I'm just sharing possible, not necessarily plausible, theories."

I took a long sip of my milk as I thought about what other reasons could explain this away. Finally, I looked at my friends. "We'll go with that for now, but my Pop-Tart-filled gut tells me there's something rotten about Chef Jonathan…something besides his cooking."

CHAPTER ELEVEN

————

Morning came entirely too early. With it, the start of another work week. I'd tossed and turned enough to convince myself that my morning workout routine had been completed. For someone who'd been an adventurer most of her life, I couldn't figure out why the thought of people in my life—myself included—picking up and moving on created such a knot in the very center of my stomach. *Or maybe that was the brief taste of Chef Jonathan's food that Bree had forced me to eat yesterday.*

Tan was waiting at the back door of the tavern when I arrived. "Hey, Lilly."

I dipped a toe in the emotional waters between us to see if the temperature was hot or cold. "Hey. You enjoy your day off?" I managed to keep from adding *without me* to the end of my question. Two points for me.

He closed the distance between us while my fingers fumbled in an effort to unlock the door. The moment his arms slid around my waist and pulled me close, I gave up any pretense of trying and melted into his frame.

"I'm sorry."

The temptation to repeat his apology hovered dangerously close to the edge of my tongue. I didn't like conflict, especially not with him. And being in his arms felt so, so good. I wasn't sure, though, what he was sorry for. For our fight? For contemplating leaving Danger Cove? For the possibility of breaking my heart? I decided to try to keep the peace while still searching for the true meaning of his apology. "You should never apologize for following your dream."

When his hand cupped my cheek and those intense blue eyes of his captured my gaze, I understood how dangerously close I was to jumping hand in hand off the love ledge with him. All of my reasons for doing so taunted me that love and commitment weren't bad things and that people successfully had normal, balanced relationships all the time. Just because my mother had taken it to the extreme didn't make it the only option. His lips were warm and soft, a blanket of contentment over my troubled soul.

All too soon, he pulled away. "I'm not apologizing for following my dream. I'm apologizing for giving you an ultimatum. It was unfair of me to lay decisions about my future in your lap. You have to do what's best for you. I have to do what's best for me. If that happens to mean us not being with each other, then…"

Though I was sure his words were meant to comfort and let me off the hook from his enthusiasm over taking our relationship to another level, I almost preferred the ultimatum to this Gandhi-inspired *what will be, will be* attitude. I put a little more distance between us. "Then what? We just shake hands, part ways, and be done?"

"That's not what I'm saying."

The desire to finally have this out and get it resolved, one way or the other, loomed large in my mind. However, I had responsibilities. The rest of the team would be arriving soon. The tavern needed to be prepared for opening. I sighed and modulated my voice to a lower, more reasonable tone. "I know. I'm just frustrated that we can't seem to figure this out. I don't want to put this discussion off, but there's work to be done."

He increased the distance between as he shook his head. His lips pressed together, waiting a beat before responding. "Sure, no problem. Just don't put it off too much longer. Chicago expects a decision from me by the end of the week, and while I'm not basing my decision on what you do or don't do, I still value your input."

This time my efforts to unlock the door worked like a charm. Too bad my efforts to unlock a little happiness again in my relationship with Tanner wasn't as effective. I nodded at his last statement and refrained from telling him my input could be summed up in two simple words: don't go.

Freddie bounced in about fifteen minutes later, right after I'd started the coffee and hot water for tea. "Guess who got an A on his first exam?"

I couldn't help but smile at his enthusiasm. "Mandi?"

He laughed. "Very funny, Boss Lady."

I didn't feel very funny lately, but if anyone could make me chuckle when I was feeling down, it was Freddie. I'd tried to get him to stop calling me by that nickname, as it was the one I reserved for Hope, but today I decided to save my energy, as I felt it was needed in other areas. "That's great, Freddie. I'm so proud of you."

The blush that covered his olive cheeks was adorable.

"Thanks." He shoved his hands into his pockets. "Okay, well, I'll go get started prepping the dining room."

"Thanks."

The rest of the team arrived with a little less enthusiasm. The tension between Tara and Clara was almost palpable. Not an angry tension—this was a band of sadness stretching between them. What was worse? I was at a loss for what to do to fix it.

Drake looked bleary eyed as he grabbed a cup and stared down the coffeepot. I suppressed a chuckle and the desire to issue him a warning that a watched pot never brews. His demeanor didn't seem to invite playful warnings today. I tried not to think about how he might take it if I had to fire him. I'd cross that bridge when I came to it. As Gram always said, "Don't borrow trouble from tomorrow. Today's is sufficient."

Mandi looked better than the other three, but not by much. "What's wrong, Mandi? You didn't get sick from our meal yesterday, did you?"

She slid her apron on and poured herself a cup of tea. "I didn't, but my mom is sick. She was up and down all night. Had to call in sick to work today. I think that's the first time in years she's missed."

"I hope she feels better." I might not be able to fix things with Tan right now or bridge the gap between Clara and Tara, but this…this I could do something about. While Mandi got ready to start her shift, I grabbed a cup of tea and stood by Tara, waiting for her to finish writing up today's specials.

"Hey, Lilly. What's up? This lineup look okay to you?"
She handed me the paper.

I offered a cursory scan of the document. Bottom line, I
trusted Tara's judgment when it came to the kitchen. "Not
okay—perfect."

She grinned from the praise. "Thank you. Is there
something I can do for you?"

Don't leave me too..."I was wondering if you had time
today, could you whip up some good ol' fashioned chicken soup
for Mandi's mom? She's not feeling well."

Tara nodded. "I'd be happy too. Best home remedy I
know of."

"Same here. If there's enough, I'll take some to Agnes
too. She's been pretty sick lately as well."

Her face scrunched up. "You don't think it's a bug going
around, do you?"

"I'm sure they're completely isolated incidents. We'll use
extra hand sanitizer and bleach today, just in case."

Tara smiled and nodded. She ran a tight and
immaculately clean kitchen. There was a strict no-germ policy
here. I left her to get started on all she had to do and headed to
the bar. I might be acting manager, but behind the bar still felt
like home. Today, I needed some of the comfort the routine
offered me.

Shortly after the lunch rush, one of my favorite people
joined me at the bar. "Hi, Maura. How are things at the bakery?"

Maura Monroe had moved into town shortly before I
did. She'd fallen in love with the town and became somewhat of
a local hero when she purchased the Cinnamon Sugar Bakery
and reopened it. I knew I had found a great deal of happiness in
her baked goods.

"Hi, Lilly. What is the lunch special today? I've been
working Heather really hard trying out new recipes. If I don't
bring some real food back, you'll find us victims of a sugar
crash."

I could think of worse ways to go. "We can't have that
happening. Where would I go for my sugar fix if something
happened to either of you?" I handed her a menu. "Today's lunch
special is pulled pork sliders, truffle fries, and summer slaw."

Her lips curled into a smile. "That sounds delish. I'll take two of those to go and a Coke while I wait."

After entering her order, I poured her drink. "Business good?"

"Business is great. Hard to keep up with the demand, but you won't hear me complaining." She propped her chin on her hand. "Tell me about this handsome new gardener you have. He's rather dark and mysterious, isn't he?"

Both qualities seemed to sum up Drake quite nicely. "That sounds about right. How do you know him?"

"Blake insisted we go back to The Pelican Bar last week to commemorate all the excitement we had there when I first got to town. Blake had met him before at the hardware store and introduced himself, figuring he might need a place to stay since he was new in town. Anyway, when I saw Drake that night, he was sitting at a corner table by himself. Though a number of women were doing their best to attract his attention. It truly was quite humorous to watch."

She'd piqued my curiosity. "What was he doing? Just drinking?"

I worried that drinking alone at a bar, along with the bottle of alcohol I'd seen in the greenhouse, could indicate Drake had a drinking problem. Of course, it could all add up to my overactive imagination.

"He was nursing a drink, but was studying something in his hand pretty intently. No idea what it was. Blake wanted to go up and say hi, but I've learned that when someone is giving off a don't-bother-me vibe, it's typically good to respect that."

She was right. I just hadn't learned to respect those vibes quite yet. Some would argue that got me into a great deal more trouble than necessary. Wanting to change the subject from my gardener, I turned the conversation in her direction. "Speaking of Blake. How is he?"

If my rumor mill fodder was accurate, Blake and Maura were somewhat of an item, even though Blake was a self-proclaimed bachelor. He was co-owner of Glover Rentals, a very popular business, especially during the height of tourist season.

"Blake is good. Too busy for his own good." Her expression transformed for a moment to schoolgirl dreamy as her thoughts obviously drifted to him. A moment later, she was back to business. "You should reach out to him once your lease expires at Hazlitt Heights. If you're looking to buy, that is. He could hook you up with a nice rental until you decide on a permanent place."

It felt a little like the universe was ganging up on me regarding my housing situation, and I fought the twinge of irritation attempting to unleash a sarcastic and inappropriate remark. Instead I smiled. "I appreciate that and will keep it in mind. I'm rarely home though, so an apartment presently equals the amount of upkeep I'm able to commit to."

Maura finished her drink and offered a wry smile. "You may be right, or maybe upkeep isn't what you're having trouble committing to. I remember, after my husband died, searching for the place I belonged. Once I found it, here in Danger Cove, it was a little scary to let go of everything I'd known for so long. But here I am, happily fulfilling the sweet tooth cravings of an entire town and the surrounding communities."

Clara brought her order from the back and placed it in front of her. "Enjoy."

Maura picked up the bag of food and placed cash on the bar to cover the check. "Thanks for the food and conversation. Just remember that, while life is an adventure, it's okay to have a home base."

She waved off the change I tried to give her and headed out before I could respond. Maybe she was right, or maybe they were all crazy. Rather than whether I should buy a home when my lease expired, the big question remained: would this still be home if everyone I cared about moved on?

CHAPTER TWELVE

———

Mandi emerged from the kitchen moments after Maura left. "Phone call for you, Lilly. It's Agnes. Sounds urgent."

Nothing like someone else's troubles to veer attention away from my own. "Okay, thanks." I turned my attention to Tanner. "Could you cover for a few? I have a phone call."

"Sure."

No smile or tease from him. Despite what he had said, I wasn't sure things would be alright no matter what happened. With nothing more to say, I sighed and simply offered, "Thanks."

I closed the door to Hope's office and exhaled slowly before picking up the phone. I prayed Agnes hadn't taken a turn for the worse. Forcing a smile to my face, I lifted the receiver and pressed the blinking red button. "Hi, Agnes. How are you feeling?"

"Lilly, thank God. What took you so long?"

"I'm at work." This time my grin was genuine. "Some of us still work, you know. My fortune wasn't quite as large as yours."

"Oh, tosh, if you hadn't given most of yours away to build that park and set up a scholarship fund, you could've managed to live a life of leisure."

Not wanting to argue, I opted for the path of least resistance. "You're right. The next time I'm left with a large inheritance, I'll save it all for myself. Now tell me how you're feeling."

"I need to see you."

The urgency in her tone had me worried. "I can come by and see you at the hospital tomorrow before work."

"No. Today. I've been discharged from the hospital. I'm home."

"Agnes, not only am I working, but Hope left me in charge. I just can't take a few hours off. People here need me."

The audible exhale in my ear stressed how much she was fighting for control of her emotions. "*I* need you, Lilly. Now please…"

"Okay, let me see what I can do."

"Don't be long." Agnes issued her final command before cutting the connection.

"You're welcome. Yes, nice talking to you too." My words wafted into the room around me with no one to hear them. Still, they felt good to say. I initiated a new call and dialed Tanner's sister, Ashley.

"Hello?"

"Hi, Ashley. It's Lilly."

"Oh, hey, Lilly. What's up?"

I felt bad asking her to come in on her day off, especially in the summer, but desperate times and all. "I need to take care of a few things this afternoon and was wondering if you could do me a favor and come in for at least a few hours and help in the dining area so that Mandi or Tan can cover the bar?"

There was a pause, a little long for my liking, but finally she spoke. "I'll get paid, right?"

"Of course. Why wouldn't I pay you?"

"Well, you did say it was a favor."

You had to love teenagers. "You're right. I did. It's a favor since I'm asking you to come in when you're not scheduled. You'll still get paid like you normally do."

"Okay, great. Be there in ten."

"Thanks." I hung up the phone feeling this conversation went far better than the one with Agnes. The smell of chicken soup wafted into the office and called to me with its siren song. I was helpless to resist.

Closing the distance between me and the savory soup, I smiled at Tara. "This smells fantastic."

Her grin widened at my compliment. "Want to taste?"

"Is Smugglers' Tavern known for their pirates?"

She laughed and ladled some soup into a cup. The chunks of white chicken, carrots, celery, and whatever those little green herbs she'd used for seasoning were bathing in a golden broth. I lifted the spoon to my lips and blew to cool it slightly. A moment later, the flavor washed over my taste buds and transported me to a happy place. "Oh, Tara…this is so good. So much better than Chef Jonathan's leftovers I was forced to eat yesterday evening."

The moment the words left my mouth, I regretted them. Tara's face moved from pride to annoyed. "Chef Jonathan is a master at what he does. It's just hard to cook in someone else's kitchen. You don't like him because he's trying to steal me away from you."

I couldn't argue with her about that. I wasn't happy with him for a number of reasons. His attempt to poach Tara, especially without considering the other half of the Dynamic Duo, did make me dislike him…a lot. There was no reason to point out to her that he was trying to steal me away too. She wouldn't be interested in that detail.

After placing the cup on the counter, I clasped both of her shoulders with my hands. "Just so there's no misunderstanding, I want you to know that I think you are one of the finest chefs to ever put on an apron. Neither Hope nor I would ever stand in the way of you following your dream, even if that took you away from us. I would miss you terribly, both your skills in the kitchen and as my friend. Having made that clear, whatever you decide to do is okay with me."

Tears glistened in her eyes, and she nodded. "Thanks, Lilly. This is so hard."

I pulled her into a quick hug. I understood the dilemma completely. A song Mandi had forced me to listen to one evening while I was hanging out at her apartment—"Should I Stay or Should I Go"—should be the theme song around here right now.

Once I'd secured the envelope of cash from a locked drawer in the desk, two containers of soup, one for Agnes and one for Mandi's mom, I filled the team in on the latest and headed out. At first I pedaled quickly, not wanting the soup to get cold, but realized that no matter how fast I went, Mrs.

Adam's soup didn't stand a chance of not having to be reheated. I knew both she and Agnes had a stove and microwave, so warming it wouldn't be a problem.

I was about halfway to Agnes's house when my phone rang. It was Vernon. "Hi!"

"Hi, Lilly. Are you outside? Sounds windy."

"I'm on my bike delivering some chicken soup to the sick." Thank goodness I'd invested in a Bluetooth headset. Otherwise my multitasking skills would seriously be put to the test.

"New service you're offering at the tavern—delivery?"

I chuckled. "No. Just an old service I offer to friends. You need me to bring you something? More scones maybe?"

"I wish, but so far I haven't earned them."

That wasn't good news. Vernon's connections had come through every time so far. "Were you able to learn anything?"

"Only that both Rico and Drake lived in Seattle at one point in time. My connection is going to reach out to someone they know in Seattle to see if anything more can be learned. I'll keep you posted."

It wasn't much at all, but I suppose a little more than I'd known before. "Thanks, Vernon. I appreciate it."

"Welcome, kiddo. Be careful out there on the roads. No speeding."

Vernon was such a kidder, at least when it came to me. I think it was the scones I supplied him with—they brought out his sweeter side. That was my story anyway, and I was sticking to it.

Ten minutes later, I arrived at Agnes's house. I knocked on the door and waited.

"Lilly? Come in."

I let myself in the front door, but stopped short at the sight before me. The living room looked like a cyclone had taken a round trip through it. Agnes might be a little messy from time to time, but I'd never seen her home in such a state of disarray. A half-empty bottle of tequila sat on the coffee table next to a glass big enough to hold at least two shots. Agnes was pacing back and forth, wearing a path in the one area of the floor not occupied with papers, pillow, or other personal items.

"Agnes, what's wrong?"

The pacing stopped long enough for her to pierce me with her tear-filled gaze. "You have to believe me. I didn't mean to do it."

"Then who is responsible for this mess, young lady?" I tried a lighthearted approach to see if I could break her out of this downward spiral she had jumped on.

The red curls flipped wildly as she shook her head from side to side. "This isn't a laughing matter, Lilly. I need your support, not your silliness."

Okay...message received. Not a time for jokes. "I'm sorry. What can I do to support you?"

She started pacing again. I decided to go on a fishing expedition. "Did Chef Jonathan say or do something to upset you?" Maybe she'd signed over half her fortune to him in a moment of weakness.

A few sniffles later, she answered, "The man is relentless, but nothing I can't handle. He comes off a bit desperate, don't you think?"

This coming from a woman who'd trashed her living room, indulged in a decent amount of tequila, and had obviously been crying. Vibrations of desperation echoed off the walls in here. She did have a point though. "He does seem fixated on getting his hands on our money."

"That seems to be going around."

Her response was mumbled, but I'd heard it. "Who else is trying to get your money?"

"You have to believe that I didn't mean to."

And we'd come full circle. This time I tried a different approach. "I'm sure you didn't, Agnes. It was an accident, right?" Whatever *it* was.

She plopped into the recliner, and the Persian cat jumped up onto her lap, demanding attention. I remembered the affection she held for her cats one of the other times I was at her house. "Does this have something to do with Rico?"

"I'd realized the ring was a fake when I'd tried to polish it a few days ago. I decided it was time for a little payback for Rico and all the grief he'd been causing me since we got home. By leaving it in the cleaning solution when I left, my goal was to stir up a bit of panic in him when he saw the ring start to dissolve."

At least now I knew at what point Agnes realized the ring was a fake. Now that she was more forthcoming, I didn't want to say or do anything to stop the flow of information. "Maybe whoever sold it to him perpetrated the fraud?" Personally, I didn't buy that theory for one millisecond, but the possibility existed.

"Sweet of you to suggest, but you and I both know that's not what happened."

I knelt down in front of her and softened my voice. "That's what friends are for."

The tears started rolling down her cheeks again. "I should have confronted him right then and there, but I was so upset I couldn't think straight. I had to get out of there before I did something I regretted."

"Sounds reasonable."

"Sounds cowardly. I wanted so badly to believe he loved me for me…not my money." Her gaze found mine. "You're lucky. You know that Tanner loved you with or without the money."

Why did everyone insist on correlating what was happening in their lives to Tanner's and my relationship? Seriously, didn't they have enough of their own problems? Good Lord knows I had enough of my own. *Yet here I am trying to get Agnes to talk about her problems, which are far worse than mine at the moment.* "So you went over to visit Clara and Tara's parents. What happened next?"

I remembered what she had told me the day it happened, but guilt has a way of changing a story depending on how much sympathy a person is looking to gain. It took a Herculean effort on my part not to supply her with the rendition she had given me that day in order to help all of this turn out to be accidental. Still…anger over Rico's betrayal might have been the final straw to the marital issues they'd been having.

"When I came home from my visit, prepared to confront him, he was unconscious on the floor. He must've gotten dizzy from the fumes, fallen, and hit his head. What are the chances a fall like that could kill you?" Her question was delivered with disbelief and a hint of anger.

My edit function managed to prevent me from telling her that apparently the chances were one hundred percent in this case. There were several burning questions I wanted to ask her, including why have me look for the ring when she knew it was a fake? Maybe she thought it might make her look guilty? Not sure, but not important right now. I handed her the envelope. "This is what I found when I was looking for your ring. I'm pretty sure it's an envelope of cash. Do you know anything about it?"

This inquiry prompted her to stand and start to pace again. Not the reaction I'd wanted. After a few minutes of pacing, she stopped and leaned against the wall as if she could no longer support herself without assistance. "It was my money, but Rico made the withdrawal."

"How do you know?"

She closed her eyes. "I might as well tell you everything so that you can help me frame it in the best way for the police."

Which meant she hadn't mentioned the cash to them when they spoke to her after they were here for their initial visit. As someone who'd withheld information to protect myself or those I loved, I couldn't really judge. "Agreed. The more I know, the more I can help you."

"I'd shared with you about my troubles in paradise. What I didn't share was that I'd begun to suspect that Rico was only after my money from almost the moment we got home. His whole demeanor changed. The way he talked to me. The way he treated me. I may be naïve when it comes to love, but I'm not entirely stupid. One plus one equals two every single time. Attractive man woos recently wealthy woman until she lets him put a ring..." She chuckled and shook her head. "Put a fake ring on her finger. The ink is barely dry on the marriage certificate when he begins to treat her like a leper in her own home."

"I'm sorry, Agnes." And I really was.

She batted away my sympathy as though it were an annoying fly getting too close. "Anyway, as I mentioned, I'm not stupid. I put alerts on my account so I'd know whenever a withdrawal had been made."

"His name was on the account? That was fast."

"He could be very convincing. Even though I suspected a less-than-honorable intent, he could get me to lower my guard long enough to get what he wanted from me. I'm not proud of it, but it's true."

"The heart does things for reason...that reason doesn't understand." I quoted from one of my favorite Disney movies, hoping she would find comfort in the words. Hey, don't judge. A wealth of wisdom can be found in *The Princess Diaries*.

"Oh, honey, it wasn't my heart I was listening to. It was all those girly parts doing their happy dance when he started playing their song."

With just a few words, she'd moved us from Disney to *Dirty Dancing*. Another Hallmark moment ruined. "Fair enough. Go on."

"I made sure I knew when he made withdrawals on the account or charges on the card. Anything less than a thousand, I didn't even pay attention to."

She definitely had more money than I did...or ever would have. I was okay with that. "So there was more than a thousand dollars in the envelope?"

"Ten thousand."

"Wow!"

She smiled. "Yes, wow."

"What was it for?" My curiosity kitty was clawing to get to the bottom of this mystery.

"I don't know. I was going to ask him, but then..."

Then he was dead. "Okay, maybe we can look through some of his things to figure out if he owed money to someone." Or maybe he'd decided to invest privately in Chef Jonathan's business to get a piece of the pie outside of Agnes, just in case things didn't work out. It didn't seem plausible given the encounter I witnessed between them that day in Charlie's kitchen, but I was just brainstorming. Which meant I was grasping at straws to try to make sense of all of this.

She shrugged. "You're welcome to look around wherever you want. I don't even care why he did it."

Now we were getting to the heart of the matter. "Just that he did it."

"Yes. Without asking or telling me. He just took the money as though it belonged to him. A few weeks with me and he already felt he could lay claim to ten thousand dollars of *my* money."

The anger had returned to her voice. "Circling back to your original claim when I arrived—the important part here is that you didn't plan to kill him, right?" The toxic fumes from the cleaning solution had been stronger than any I'd ever encountered. If she had realized the mixture was toxic or had added more to the mix before she left, that could spell trouble.

The intensity of Agnes's gaze drove an arrow straight through the thin veil of reasonable doubt I was trying to weave on her behalf. "Did I want him to die? No. Did I want him to suffer? You bet your best bottle of tequila I did."

CHAPTER THIRTEEN

Several moments of stunned silence stood between Agnes and me as I processed her words. Once that was complete, I gestured to the dining room table in the adjacent room. "Maybe we should sit down."

She grabbed the tequila and a glass and followed me without saying a word. She downed the equivalent of a double shot before she continued her story. "I added some extra ammonia to the mixture right before I left. I figured the fumes would make him cough, hopefully make him sick, and turn his insides out the way he'd been doing to mine since we returned from the cruise."

The way she delivered her agenda chilled the blood in my veins a few degrees. I smiled a little to soften the impact of my words. Agnes was obviously not a woman to be trifled with, and I didn't want to get on her bad side, especially when she and I were alone. "Maybe work on your delivery before sharing that with Detective Marshall."

Agnes nodded. "Once he recovered a bit, I was going to show him the fake ring and enjoy the look on his face when I let him know I was going to see an attorney to file for a divorce."

"Had you already called and made the appointment?"

"Of course. Why?"

"Because if his death is ruled a homicide, they're going to start looking into everything. It won't take them long to discover you'd decided to file for divorce." She'd be lucky if Detective Pizza Guy didn't lock her up and throw away the key on that point alone.

"You've forgotten I worked at the police department for years. The fact I had an appointment helps rather than hurts me." Agnes smiled at her revelation.

The more I learned about Agnes's story and the steps she'd taken, the more it made me feel like premeditation might be on the table. "How so?"

"If I was going to divorce him, why would I try to kill him?"

"Valid point." Though I could think of a few reasons, including his taking advantage of her. It was also difficult to move past the logic that it appeared her actions, accidental or not, did most likely result in his death.

Agnes took another long sip of tequila before slouching back in her chair and closing her eyes. "Why couldn't the idiot have just thrown up where he sat? If he'd done that instead of trying to get up, he'd probably be alive today."

I shook my head and took her hand. "Again, Agnes, not the best way to frame your story. Right now the police believe this was an accident. And it was…sort of…we just need to practice your statement a little before you give it. I have to get back to work, but why don't you work on your version of events and search through Rico's things to see if you can find anything that might explain the ten grand. That could prove very helpful." I left out the part that her story needed all the help it could get right now.

My words perked her up. She stood and grabbed her purse. "I promise I'll do that later. Maybe you can come by after work and help? I think what will make me feel better is a little retail therapy. I'm going to head to Seattle. Can I pick you up anything while I'm there?"

Unbelievable. "No, thank you. I'll talk to you later." I'd thought about voicing my concern over how much she'd had to drink and then driving, but before I could say anything, she was muttering something about finding the right app to get a driver. At least she hadn't totally lost her senses.

Confident that Agnes wasn't going to get behind the wheel of a car, I grabbed the other container of soup and headed to Hazlitt Heights. One more delivery and I could return to the safety of my bar. Despite the difficult situation with Agnes, I couldn't help but smile as I thought about the fact that I considered it *my* bar. Could I find that feeling somewhere else? Somewhere without Tanner? The smile faded. No doubt he was a big part of the happiness I'd found here in Danger Cove.

My apartment building came into view. The three-story building was well maintained, simple, and clean. A few flowers added a splash of color to the beds out in front of the mowed lawn. The landscaping wasn't fancy, but you could tell some effort was being put into making the place look nice. I knew I'd certainly stayed in far worse places as I'd made my way across the good ol' United States. New York to Washington—from sea to shining sea. It had been a great adventure, which led me here.

I knocked on the door of Mandi and her mother's apartment. "Ms. Adams? It's Lilly. I brought some soup. Can I come in?"

A minute or so later the door opened. I managed to keep my gasp from escaping. She looked terrible. Pale skin, tired eyes, slow movements. I really, really hoped she wasn't contagious. I lifted the container. "Homemade chicken noodle soup requested by your daughter, created by Tara, delivered by me."

My statement brought a small smile to her colorless lips. "Thanks, Lilly. That was very sweet of all of you."

"Let me heat it up for you. Looks like you could use a little nourishment."

"Are you sure?"

I lifted my free hand over my heart and feigned hurt. "I do know how to operate a microwave. That might be the extent of my kitchen appliance know-how, but I have lots of experience with various makes and models. You have a seat, and I'll take care of this."

She was far more compliant than Agnes had been during my most recent visit and followed my instructions. Since I'd hung out with Mandi many times at her place, I had a basic knowledge of where things were. A few minutes later, I placed a steaming cup of soup in front of my patient. Ms. Adams obliged me by taking a bite. I couldn't wait to hear her reaction. "Isn't it just amazing? The flavors wash over every taste bud. It's feel-good magic right there in a cup." I giggled at my statement. "I think being around all these chefs is turning me into a foodie."

Ms. Adams smiled, but shrugged. "I'm sure it is all those things. Sadly, it could taste like dirt, and I wouldn't know the difference."

"Why? What's wrong?"

"This virus has affected my taste buds. Can't really taste anything." She lifted the cup for another few sips. "I'll be sure and save some though. When I'm better, I'd love to experience a little of that magic you mentioned. Thank you all for being so thoughtful."

I gave her a quick hug—hopefully not long enough to allow the germs to jump from her to me. "Feel better."

My legs pumped hard to get me back to the tavern. I felt bad being away so long. There'd been no calls for help or even *Where are you?* texts, so there was a confidence that the team had it all under control. While my body did its job, my mind focused on the fact Ms. Adams couldn't taste anything due to her illness. Maybe that was how Allyson was able to eat Jonathan's food yesterday without spitting it out. She couldn't taste it. Made sense. I knew she was love sick, but didn't think that would make those important little buds on your tongue go into hiatus. Whatever she had—I hoped I wouldn't get it.

Tan was busy at the bar when I returned. Dinner rush was in full swing. I slid my apron over my head as I moved beside him. "Why don't you take a break? Thanks for helping out."

He shrugged. "That's what friends are for."

Something about the way he said *friends* bound all the loose emotional cords in my stomach into a double constrictor knot. I'd learned a lot about knots from some of the sailors passing through who had stopped in for a meal or a pint. The constrictor knot was the most difficult one to untie.

Tan left for his break without another word. Drake arrived a minute later. "Hey, Boss. My shift is finished for the day. I checked with Tara, and she said they were all set in the kitchen. I think Tan's kid sister is assisting or something. Okay for me to be done, or do you need help?"

A quick cursory glance around the tavern showed everything to be in order—along with a manageable number of patrons. "I think we're good. Thanks for offering. Can I get you something to drink?"

He pointed to the bottle of Tsunatka tequila—Agnes's poison of choice. "I'll have a shot of that before I go."

I picked up the bottle. "You sure? I can't give you the employee discount on alcohol. A shot runs thirty-five dollars."

Drake flashed a handsome grin. "Make it a double. My mom sent me an early birthday present with some cash. I want to celebrate. I wish Agnes was here to celebrate with me. I'd buy her a shot."

I measured the liquid into the shot glass. "I'm sure she'd love that. She was disappointed that Rico didn't share her love of tequila."

The alcohol disappeared in quick order as he downed the shot in one smooth motion. "Just a single shot this time. Good thing I'm walking home." He laughed.

In an effort to try to get him to open up and share a little more, I decided to give him an early birthday present. "This one is on me. Happy early birthday."

"Thanks. That's very nice of you." He jerked his head in the direction of the door where Tanner usually stood to provide security. "I hope he realizes how good he's got it. Women like you are hard to find."

My face heated at his compliment, but I needed to stop this before it got started. "He does realize it. We're very happy, thank you."

His response sounded like a cross between a snort and a guffaw, but I ignored him. When I didn't take the bait to share about my relationship with Tanner, he continued. "Have they learned anything more about Rico's death?"

"What do you mean?"

"Was it ruled accidental?"

I rinsed a few glasses and put the bottle of tequila back on the shelf. "Last I heard, they were still waiting on the autopsy results." His curiosity could be explained by the need to feed the small-town gossip mill, but I was still convinced he'd known Rico. I decided I could play the curiosity game. "Why, have you heard something?"

He shrugged and leaned back on the barstool. "I just think it's curious that not even twenty-four hours after his death, his ex and a man he obviously didn't like were seen strolling on the pier holding hands."

He made a valid point. "I agree. I ran into them yesterday over at Ocean View. They did seem to be happy. What makes you think Allyson and Rico were together in the past?" I'd surmised the same after hearing their exchange at brunch on Sunday, but since Drake wasn't there, I had no idea how he would know.

"Clara filled me in. She was hanging out on the bench out back during her break. She was anxious to talk about the whole thing, so I let her." He cracked a grin. "Not only am I a great with my hands, I'm a good listener too."

I wasn't sure if he was trying to flirt (ugh!) or was referencing his skills in the garden. Either way, I still wouldn't take the bait. "I'm sure she appreciated the listening ear. Do you think it was a love triangle or something going on between the three of them?" I wasn't sure how much Clara had shared, so I decided to dangle a little fishing bait of my own. From what I witnessed, Allyson hated Rico. Experience had taught me that hate that strong often emerged as a result of loving someone with that same intensity before things went horribly wrong.

My question caused him to arch an eyebrow. "What makes you think I would know anything about that?"

Since I didn't want to bring up the background check and the subsequent info I'd received from Vernon until I had the complete picture, I fabricated the tiniest of white lies. It wasn't even a half lie…more like a quarter, maybe even a tenth. Yeah, let's go with a tenth of a lie. "When I spoke with Allyson, she mentioned she was originally from Seattle. You listed a previous address in Seattle on some of your paperwork. Agnes told me Rico was from Seattle. I thought maybe your paths had crossed at some point."

He looked at me with an odd expression—one I couldn't place—before grinning at me. "Seattle is a lot bigger than Danger Cove. It's not like everyone knows everyone…or their business…like they try to do here." He pulled out his credit card. "I'll cash out. Thanks."

My fishing expedition hadn't gleaned me any more results than his had. Well, you couldn't blame us for trying. Of course, my bait had tipped the karma scale in the negative direction thanks to my little white lies and cost me forty bucks. My internal lie detector might not be fully calibrated, but I was certain Drake knew something about Allyson that he wasn't telling me.

He signed the slip. "Thanks for the birthday shot. Have a nice evening."

"You too."

"Hey, Lilly, how's my mom doing? Did she like the soup?" Mandi emerged from the kitchen, an empty dish bin in her hands.

I recounted my visit for her. "She said to let everyone know how thoughtful it was of us to bring her the soup, even if she couldn't taste it."

Mandi's nose wrinkled in an adorable fashion as she scrunched up her face. "That's too bad. I had some during my break. It was so good."

"Agreed. Maybe I should get Tara to add it to the menu this fall. Hot soups are always a crowd pleaser. Oh, it did make me think that maybe Allyson was sick, and that's why she couldn't taste Jonathan's cooking."

Mandi chuckled at my statement, but then a serious look crossed her face. The look that told me she'd just thought of some detail I hadn't. Which, by the way, happened a lot. Trivia and details were her thing. "What's up, Mandi? What are you thinking?"

She leaned over the bar and lowered her voice. "It's probably crazy…"

"I thought that we did crazy, you and me. Don't go getting sane on me now."

"What if it was Chef Jonathan who lost his ability to taste?"

CHAPTER FOURTEEN

———

Mandi's statement, simple yet profound, gave me pause. She continued with her thought process. "It makes sense when you think about it."

"How so?" I could probably figure it out, but if she'd already done the mental math, no sense in me recalculating.

"He was reluctant to cook the meal from the beginning, right?"

"Right."

"But Agnes is relentless and wouldn't even consider giving him money without tasting the product first, so he had no choice."

I nodded my head and picked up on her train of thought. "But he knew if *he* tried to cook the meal, Agnes and I might sense that something was off, especially since we were expecting perfection. I'm not sure what happened at Bree's the other night. Maybe her spices really were old and useless or maybe her chicken really was starting to go bad. Who knows. Regardless, delivering anything short of perfection at the brunch could potentially sink his hopes of securing new investors for his business."

Mandi's blue eyes sparkled like freshly polished sapphires. "Exactly. He couldn't have that, so he insisted that Tara and Clara assist him."

Tiny goose bumps prickled my skin. "Clara told me that morning that she and Tara had done all the work. Even said he was testing them when it came to the flavor combinations. When I ate my dish, it reminded me of their style and presentation." Trust me, I'd eaten enough food prepared by them to know.

"Makes sense. He needed them so his secret would remain safe."

Some customers chose that moment to walk in and take a seat in one of the booths. Mandi sighed. "Guess we'll have to continue this later."

I checked on the few patrons at the bar and started some of my cleaning routine. The more I could get done now, the less I'd have to do at closing time. The circular motion of the cloth against the stainless steel of the sink area helped me think. If it was true that Chef Jonathan had lost his ability to taste, the stakes for him would have reached new heights. It would be a long, hard fall if word of this got out. *Assuming it's true.*

Bottom line—it was the only thing that could explain away his odd behavior. Desperate men do desperate things. Rico had issued the threat about Agnes's money. So one had to ask: would Jonathan kill to get it? That was a question I'd need to answer…and soon.

I tried to determine the best way to obtain that answer— short of asking him—which I didn't feel would go over well. Given the man was an expert with knives, I decided a head-on approach would most likely end with me on the wrong side of a razor-sharp edge.

Before I could formulate an alternate approach, Allyson walked in with a man dressed like he'd stepped out of the center of *Vogue* magazine. In addition to his finely tailored suit, he sported a very unique accessory: an onyx and silver cane, which gleamed in the artificial light. Was it customary to polish a cane? Interestingly, he didn't appear to have a limp of any kind leading me to believe it was a decorative accent to the outfit. To top off his model-worthy look, he had a clean-cut square jaw and hair as black as night. It was his smile, though, that caught my attention. It lit up the room and upped the swoon factor for single women by at least ten decibels.

Allyson and Mr. Vogue walked directly to the bar. "Hi, Lilly. This is Steven Sinclair. He's Jonathan's business partner."

The smile on her face as she looked up into those mesmerizing eyes of his struck chords of adoration. My immediate thought was that maybe *he* was the mystery man she'd cheated with. Though I didn't condone cheating, no jury of her peers would ever convict her once an eight-by-ten glossy of Mr. Sinclair was admitted into evidence.

Mr. Sinclair and I shook hands. "Pleasure to meet you. Can I get you something to drink?"

"Tequila, please. Straight up."

I pointed to the row of tequila bottles. "Pick your poison," I offered with a grin.

Without hesitation, he chose Agnes's favorite. Not only was I going to have to try this, as it seemed to be a favorite for those who could afford to be selective, I was going to have to order some more. "Great choice. Would you like it chilled?"

"Please."

"Anything for you, Allyson?"

She shook her head, but then added, "Could I get some water with lemon?"

"Sure." While I prepared their drinks, I noticed Allyson's gaze searching the restaurant, continually returning to the door to the kitchen. "Looking for someone?"

"Steven would like a few minutes of Tara's time if you can spare her."

Every fiber of my being wanted to tell her to get out of my bar and take her smooth-talking tequila drinker with her. But I'd promised Tara I wouldn't stand in her way. A promise was a promise, especially when made to a close friend. I poured Steven's chilled tequila into a shot glass and put it in front of him. "Dinner rush is over, so she should be able to spare some time. Let me check."

He leaned his head back and downed the shot in one smooth swallow. Definitely not his first trip to tequila town. He placed the shot glass back on the bar and smiled. "Chilled to the perfect temperature. Thank you."

I shrugged and nodded with a slight smile. "It's what I do. Let me check on Tara."

In the kitchen, I found my chef with her head in our large, commercial refrigerator. The clipboard in her hand indicated to me she was doing inventory. Guess it had been a slow night for orders. Clara was chopping vegetables with a vengeance. Ashley was washing a pan with her head down. No conversation. No banter. Not good.

"Everything okay in here?"

"Yes." They all answered in unison without looking up, which screamed: *everything is not okay.*

Tara continued her work in the fridge, but asked, "You have an order?"

"No, but there's someone out front who wants to see you."

"Who?"

"Steven Sinclair. He's Chef Jonathan's business partner."

Tara turned to look at me—finally. Her eyes sparkled with excitement while her mouth twisted downward in regret. "He wants to see me now?" She chanced a quick glance at Clara, who had increased the velocity of her chopping on the hapless veggies.

I gestured to the refrigerator. "If you can tear yourself away from inventory, yes."

"Okay then." She closed the door and smoothed her apron.

"Grab a soda or tea and pick a booth in the back. You'll have some privacy there."

Tara nodded. "Thanks, Lilly."

Once she exited the kitchen, I moved a little closer to Clara. Not too close. She was upset and possessed a very sharp knife with the skills to use it. "If your vegetables can spare you for a few minutes, why don't you come help me at the bar?"

The chopping stopped, and she put the knife down. "What help could you possibly need at the bar from me?"

I reached out to put my hand on her shoulder and squeezed gently. "I'm sure some oranges or lemons could be sliced."

"I appreciate what you're trying to do, Lilly. I'm not sure I want to watch as my sister seals a deal that will take her away from me." She plopped down on a stool we kept near the chopping station. "I guess I knew there might come a time when we wouldn't be together every day. I just didn't think it would happen so soon."

I slid my arm around her shoulders and pulled her into a half hug. "Change isn't easy, especially if it means we might be separated from those we love."

She leaned against me. "My head knows you're right. My heart disagrees. We've been together since the beginning. Actually, since before the beginning."

"She's torn too. I can see part of her wants to stay here with you. She's conflicted. We never know where life will take us. I never would have guessed I would end up here with all of you. As much as I miss my home and friends in New York, I wouldn't want to change a thing now."

"What if I'm not as good as she is or if I'm not as good without her?" The emotion in her voice tugged at all the insecurities I secretly harbored every time there was a major change in my life.

I pulled away and turned her so that she was looking directly at me. "I want you to know I have absolute faith in your abilities, but I understand where you're coming from. I feel the same way every time Hope calls to say she's staying away longer. Bottom line though, you'll never know until you try."

Clara sniffed and nodded her head. "Okay. Thanks for the pep talk. Maybe I'll go slice some lemons and oranges for you."

"Sounds good. I'm going to grab a quick cup of tea and will be right out."

Once Clara left the kitchen, Ashley looked up from her dishes. "Is that the same pep talk you gave my brother to encourage him to leave me and Mom?"

Ugh. I'd almost forgotten about Ashley being in the room. She wasn't typically this quiet. "No, it's the pep talk I give myself every time my heart rips in two at the thought of him leaving. I told him that he needed to pursue whatever makes him happy. I can't…won't stand in his way."

"You are such an idiot."

Always what a boss wanted to hear from one of her employees. "Is there a specific reason you're risking insubordination, or am I an idiot in general?" She and I'd had our differences in the past due to my relationship with her brother, but we'd been getting along reasonably well since I offered her the job at the tavern.

She dried her hands and tossed the towel on the counter. "*You* make him happy. As much as I hate to admit it, he's happier when he's with you. Ugh! You have no idea how much I hate letting those words out of my mouth. The only reason he's even considering moving halfway across the United States is because you're too scared to move forward even the tiniest of steps. He's not asking you to marry him, just take the next logical step in your relationship. You won't even officially call him your boyfriend. Seriously, can you blame him for thinking you're not as invested in this as he is? Why don't you take your own advice and realize that you'll never know if this thing you two have is going to work unless you at least try."

I opened my mouth to respond, but no words would form. She was right—a fact I hated and would bite my own tongue to prevent from saying out loud. What was worse? I knew down deep in my gut that if Tanner left, I'd have no one to blame but myself.

Before I could wallow in my growing pit of despair, my phone buzzed. The caller ID showed it was Agnes. Perfect. She was probably calling me to come to Seattle and bail her out of another mess. Who knew one news article could bind two people together so tightly? I looked at Ashley. "I have to take this, but we'll talk more soon."

"Whatever. There's been too much talk. Time for some action."

Ignoring her comment, I made my way into the office. "Hi, Agnes. Everything okay?"

"Oh, Lilly, everything is a mess."

"What's wrong? What happened?" I had a distinct feeling of déjà vu. Like we'd started a conversation or two like this before.

"Detective Marshall just called. They're ruling Rico's death a homicide."

CHAPTER FIFTEEN

———

I skipped the tea and used the time to talk Agnes off the ledge. Thankfully, this ledge was constructed of jumbled emotions rather than several stories of brick and mortar. Another bonus to a small town—no buildings tall enough to create a suicide-level event. I refused to consider the nearby cliffs and shuddered when I thought about how terrifying a fall into the swirling depths would be. I'd faced that possibility once when someone had not been too happy with my meddling. Never wanted to do that again.

The fact they hadn't charged Agnes with anything yet helped. She promised me she'd come straight home and start looking through Rico's things to find something to explain the large withdrawal. We both hoped she could find it before the police decided a more thorough search of her premises was needed. They'd asked her to come down to the station tomorrow to review her statement and answer questions.

Thankfully, she wasn't a suspect at this time. They were going to use her to start their fishing expedition. I harbored no doubts they'd be knocking on my door again soon as well. With that in mind, I'd promised to come over to her place after work and help her in whatever way I could to prepare. *Note to self, take some gloves to wear.* Tara always kept a stock of latex gloves in the kitchen. They would come in handy to prevent me from being tossed under that guilty bus again. I still had a few tire tracks on me from the last time.

A small sigh escaped my lungs. I always tried to be the best friend I could be. I'd even gone what I felt was above and beyond for Agnes. She'd been kind to me when my mother had been arrested. Because of that, I wanted to repay her kindness, but even with the best of intentions, I wasn't sure I could help her out of this tangled mess she'd gotten herself caught up in. I feared once she *did* give her statement, they'd stop looking for other potential targets. I also couldn't help but think the envelope of cash *had* to have something to do with this whole mess.

I made my way back to the bar. Clara was slicing my oranges and lemons, but the intensity I had witnessed in the kitchen had decreased by several notches. Her head was down, but she managed to occasionally bring Tara and Steven into her line of sight. I imagined the invisible cords that bound Clara and Tara together were even stronger than the ones that had kept my stomach in knots since Tan had mentioned his possible move to Chicago.

"How you doin'?" I whispered to Clara as I moved closer.

"I've seen him before." She kept her voice very low and didn't look up. It was odd, but I decided to play along.

"Where?"

"At Charlie's Cove the morning of the brunch. He was outside waiting for Allyson." She looked up and smiled shyly. "He's hard to miss. Plus, you don't normally see people with canes around here."

Mr. Vogue must consider the cane a necessary accessory regardless of when and where he was. Odd, but I couldn't argue that it seemed to work for him. "Agreed on all accounts. So what were they doing?"

She resumed slicing. "They were just talking, but they seemed pretty intense."

"Intense as in romantic?"

She shrugged. "I spend too much time in the kitchen to be sure. Vegetables and spices make sense to me. All that emotional mumbo-jumbo not as much. I don't think so though. More like they were planning something. They were so intent on each other they didn't even notice me."

This was an interesting development. Now that Rico's death had been ruled a homicide, Jonathan had officially moved to the top of my suspect list. Allyson certainly had some motive of her own. I couldn't ignore the fact that Steven also had a vested interest in Jonathan's success. As his business partner, he would understand the dire financial implications if the chef had lost his ability to taste. Sex, money, and love were among the most powerful motivators for murder. Jealousy could factor in as an added complication with any of those three.

"Did they leave together?"

She shook her head. "No, but they both turned in the same direction."

"Toward Ocean View?" That was where they were staying, or at least Allyson was, so it made sense. However, Agnes had mentioned seeing Allyson near her house when she'd gone to visit her neighbors right before Rico had ended up dead.

"No. They headed in the opposite direction."

Which just happened to be the part of town Agnes lived in. "Okay, good to know. Thanks, Clara." I let my gaze drift over the patrons sitting at the bar, not that there were many this time of night. It was a weekday after all. Everyone's glass had enough, and they were engaged in conversation with each other. Allyson wasn't among the guests at the bar any longer. "Did you see where Allyson went?"

"Ladies' room, I assume." Clara tossed the cut-up fruit into the proper bins. "I'm going to head back to the kitchen and get started on the nightly closing routine. Thanks for letting me be out here for a few."

"No problem. Hang in there. We both have to trust this will all work out for the best."

Clara offered a small smile. "I like your optimism."

No sooner had Clara left the bar than Allyson returned. "Want me to freshen up your water?"

She shook her head. "No, thank you. I just want to go home. I came for Jonathan, and we've at least started on the road to reconciliation. Time to get what he needs and go home. Life is waiting for us in San Francisco."

"So you got what you wanted?" It was a leading question with a little bait attached. I really hoped she would at least nibble.

"I wanted Jonathan, so yes."

"And Jonathan wants Agnes's money."

"And yours," she added with a smile. "Of course, he also wants you and Tara too."

I wasn't sure that he did. I saw it more of a way to entice me to invest. "That's a long list of wants. To be honest, it sends a message of desperation rather than celebration about his new venture. Desperate men do things they wouldn't normally do."

My words hit their mark, and her gaze riveted to mine. "Such as?"

I leaned forward and whispered since I didn't want to share this tidbit of information with everyone within earshot. "Such as kill Rico. I've learned his death was ruled a homicide. Since you know Jonathan far better than I do, would he kill to fulfill that list of wants?" Admittedly, it was not a well-thought-out way to reveal what I'd learned. Especially if I was looking for a confession. There was a reason I chose the restaurant business to make my living rather than law enforcement.

She finished her water and tossed a couple bills on the bar. "I'll give you one thing, Lilly. You have a very creative imagination. Stop looking for shadows where they don't exist. You're being given a once-in-a-lifetime opportunity. Don't blow it."

Allyson's and my views differed on what constituted that once-in-a-lifetime gig. "And if I refuse?"

She laughed. "You're an idiot."

Second time in one day I'd been called an idiot. This one trend I wanted reversed. Before I could respond, she mimicked my move from earlier and leaned in closer. "I tell you what. For fun, if you can come up with one shred of evidence or even a theory about Jonathan's so-called desperate actions, I'll be happy to listen. If for no other reason than small towns bore me and I'd love some entertainment."

My fists clenched at her uppity arrogance. I hadn't liked her much before, and that scale was tipping quickly into the danger zone. I knew I'd regret the next words out of my mouth, but a girl could only be called an idiot so much before her self-restraint went on hiatus. "I tell *you* what. Maybe I'm focusing on the wrong person. You reeked of desperation when you came into Charlie's that morning, begging for Jonathan to take you back. Maybe you knew Rico stood in the way of Jonathan getting Agnes to invest. It was no secret you hated Rico, so you killed him. Two birds. One stone. That's how it gets done in small towns."

The fact I didn't call her a witch with a capital *B* proved I still possessed some modicum of restraint. I deserved ice cream—with chocolate sauce. Yes, that was how this idiot would reward herself for getting through this insult-filled day.

Fire blazed in Allyson's eyes at my hypothesis surrounding her activities and implied guilt. If she was a killer, I'd just moved myself a little more in the center of her target. Maybe I would add some whipped cream to my ice cream and chocolate sauce. Life was short...very short if you made a habit of provoking possible killers.

Her lips pressed into a thin line before she whirled on her heels toward Steven. "I'm leaving. See you back at the Ocean View."

Steven stood and shook Tara's hand (not a good sign as far as I was concerned) before waving to Allyson. "We're all finished. I'll ride back with you."

"I'll be in the car."

Steven hurried after her, his long black accessory trailing behind him as he tried to catch up with her. From this angle, it looked a little bent. How odd—guess I had been paying attention to other details when he arrived. At least I could be certain that once Allyson tattled to her boyfriend, the offer for a job, real or not, would be rescinded. I was pretty sure they would still want my money though. Jonathan might be rekindling his relationship with Allison, but just because she was upset with me wouldn't change the fact he'd still want the investment dollars. I suspected Jonathan was far more loyal to the almighty dollar than he was to his on-again, off-again cheating girlfriend.

Tara walked by me toward the kitchen. I had to ask. "Good talk?"

She shrugged. "He made it sound all sunshine and roses. Even I know life isn't like that. Especially life in the kitchen of a new restaurant."

"Still undecided then?"

Tara nodded. "He wants an answer by end of business tomorrow though."

"That means your answer is due by ten in the evening, right?" I grinned. Technically, that was the end of *our* business day.

She laughed. "That's right. At least that detail buys me a little more time."

The smile faded off my face. "You need to talk to her." Tara knew, without me saying, that I was referring to her other half, Clara. "She wants to be happy for you. She's just sad at the thought of not being with you every day. I'd offer to sweeten the pot and give you a promotion to keep you, but you're already head chef. And I'm sure we couldn't match their salary, so I'll just say again, we would hate to lose you, but understand if you want to spread your wings and fly."

She gave me a quick hug. "Thanks, Lilly. Now back to work for me."

* * *

I locked the back door after completing the final checks. Mandi waited patiently for me. "You sure you don't want me to come with you? I'm not sure you should be alone with Agnes." Mandi's worried expression did nothing to ease the typhoon of turmoil twisting in my gut.

"I want you to come with me, but you need to be with your mom."

She sighed. "I know you're right, but that doesn't stop me worrying about you."

"What dangerous situation is she heading into this time?" Tanner's voice startled both of us.

"Oh, hey, Tan. Didn't realize you were still here." Mandi crossed her arms and gave him what I would characterize as a disappointed glare. "Not that you joined in enough today for us to even realize you were at work."

"I have a lot on my mind."

"And the rest of us don't?" She shook her head and unlocked her bike. "See you later, Lilly."

Mandi might be small, but she moved her bike from stationery to flying in a matter of seconds. Yeah, I didn't blame her. It wasn't much fun being around Tan and me lately. He moved closer and took my hand. "Where are you going? Should I be worried?"

I squeezed his hand tighter, not wanting to let go. "Just over to see Agnes. She needs help going through some of Rico's things."

"Want company? We could leave your bike here. If I had Mom's truck, I'd bring it with us."

Thoughts of the smooth leather interior of his cherry red Mustang and all the fun we'd had in that car dispelled a little of the gloom hanging out in my heart the past few days. "You sure?"

"As long as you don't think Agnes will mind." He led me with our clasped hands toward his car even as he made the statement.

"Are you kidding? One ounce of that Tanner charm and she'll send me home so that she can have quality time alone with you." Personally, I'd like some quality time alone with him.

We reached his vehicle, but instead of opening the door, he sandwiched me between him and the cool metal. Hmmm, trapped between muscle car and muscle man…I could live with that. His face—more importantly his lips—were scant inches away from mine. The desire to kiss him infused every fiber of my being, shutting out concern for anything and anyone else.

"Have you been thinking about us?" The whispered question threatened my little slice of heaven. What was it Ashley had said? Enough words, time for action. I wanted the action of his lips pressed against mine.

Not wanting to lose the possibility of the moment, I reached around his neck and pulled him closer. "You're always in my thoughts."

He kissed the tip of my nose. Umm, about an inch lower would be so much better.

"You know what I mean."

Might as well be honest now rather than delaying the inevitable. I'd already promised myself an ice cream sundae with enough toppings to send me into a sugar-induced coma. "I don't want you to go."

His smile almost made me forget the rest of what I needed to say. However, my eyes must've given me away, even in the dim lighting outside the tavern. He pulled back a little. "But…"

I sighed and laid my head on his shoulder. The solid beating of his heart clicked off the paces of the demise of our relationship. "But I can't ask you to stay." *Even though I want to…* Despite his promise that he wouldn't base his decision on whether we moved forward in our relationship or not, I knew in my heart he would pass up the job opportunity if I could move past my fears and make our relationship official. Whether that meant calling him my boyfriend, giving him a key to my place, or buying a home to prove I had every intention of settling down here, I was sure any of those would work. It sounded so simple—well, everything except the buying of a house—when I broke it down like that. I hated that my fears, phobias, whatever you wanted to call them, prevented me from just melting into his arms and agreeing to all of it. I would still pray every night that he stayed, but that would need to be my secret.

I lifted my head, hoping he'd still be interested in our lips meeting in a glorious kiss. Instead, his forehead rested against mine.

"Why do you have to be so noble? You could just tell me you want me so much that you can't live without me and that the thought of me leaving is too terrible to contemplate."

"Nobility is one of my best qualities…or have you forgotten?" The rest of his statement rang with such brutal honesty that I couldn't tease, not even a little.

He reached around me, completely foregoing the kind of kiss I'd been wanting all day rather than the little pecks we'd been exchanging lately, and opened the door. "Come on, noble Lilly. Agnes awaits."

I slid onto the comfortable leather, relishing the softness. The engine roared to life, and for a moment, life felt normal again. I still didn't know what I would do if Tanner left. That was not true. I did know. I'd release the stronghold on my tear ducts to create a mini Niagara Falls on my face and gain at least ten pounds from all the ice cream I'd consume. That sounded like a good plan for the first few days. After that, only time would tell.

We were almost to Agnes's house when my phone buzzed. "Hi, Agnes. We're pulling in to your drive now."

"Hurry, Lilly. I think I'm going to be sick."

The moment Tan put the car into park, I jumped out and ran to her front door. It was open. I burst inside expecting to find her writhing on the floor in pain. Instead, she was sitting at her dining room table with an open bottle of tequila. I swear, if she was drunk...

"You don't look sick, Agnes. What's with the panic call?" Her theatrics had worn me down to one last nerve, and presently, she was grinding into it with her heels.

She pushed a piece of paper toward me. "I found this by the kitchen door. Whoever left it must have slipped it through the pet door while I was away from home."

I lifted the document, and Tanner moved next to me so that we could read it together: *Leave $250,000 in a duffel bag in the trash bin behind Smugglers' Tavern at eleven tomorrow evening, or the police will be informed that you killed your husband.*

CHAPTER SIXTEEN

———

"This doesn't make any sense." Of all the things I was thinking, that was what I said out loud.

Despite the situation, Tan chuckled. "I dunno, Lilly. Seems pretty clear to me."

Agnes crossed her arms and harrumphed. "I agree with Mr. Montgomery. Ranks right up there with crystal clear if you ask me."

I raised my hands in surrender. "Hear me out. Why only ask for a quarter of a million dollars? A duffel bag will hold close to two million if you use larger bills."

"Do I even want to know how you know such a thing?" Agnes rolled her eyes before taking another sip of her tequila.

"You've met Mandi, my BFF, right? Cute redhead with a penchant for trivia. It's not like she turns that off when we're hanging out together. You have no idea how much trivia transfer has occurred between her brain and mine."

Tan smiled. "You have a point. Okay, so given Agnes's highly publicized fortune, it does make you wonder why only ask for a quarter of a million."

"Let's sit down and try to think about this a little." Tanner and I moved to the table, on opposite sides of Agnes, who remained at the head. I grabbed a piece of paper and pen from my purse. Knew that would come in handy someday.

"My husband was murdered and not by me. That's fact number one I want you to write down." Agnes started our brainstorming session out with that little tidbit.

"Not intentionally anyway." It slipped out. I couldn't help it.

"Lilly!" Tanner's surprised expression was priceless.

Agnes stood, taking her glass with her and went to stand next to the mahogany china cabinet filling one wall. "No, she's right. Depending on his cause of death, I may be prime suspect number one."

This was one puzzle I should be able to solve right away. I pulled my phone out and texted my favorite Danger Cove police officer. I hoped he would be awake and call me. A minute later, my phone buzzed. "Hi, Officer Faria. Sorry to bother you so late. I'm with Agnes and have you on speakerphone. She's really nervous about giving her statement tomorrow to Detective Marshall." I'd purposely avoided referring to Marshall as Pizza Guy, as I didn't want to start the conversation off on a bad note.

"Don't worry, Agnes. These are routine questions in order to verify the information you gave on your statement from the day of the incident. We want to try to identify who might have wanted to hurt your husband."

If the look on Agnes's face was any indication, his words had not eased her worry at all. "Thank you for sharing that. Can I ask what they found in the autopsy to change it from accidental death to homicide? Agnes is also seriously considering getting rid of her table if that's what caused...you know." It was a stretch, but mostly true. Agnes might get rid of her table, especially if they found something besides asphyxiation, which led to a head-table combination, which preceded death.

There was a pause, but not so long that the butterflies in my stomach felt the need to start flapping. "Agnes, you can keep that beautiful table...unless you'd like to sell it to me. I love the rich mahogany, and it would be just the right size for when all my family comes in."

I cleared my throat to get him back on track.

"Right, well, anyway. The wound on Rico's head was not consistent with impact from any part of the table. Plus, no varnish, fibers, or any other materials that would be found on the surface of a table were present in the wound. Something else had to have killed him. We're not sure what though. They're still investigating. All we can determine is that the weapon was blunt and packed a mighty punch."

That narrowed it down to a few thousand possible items. "Okay, thanks so much. Good luck with your investigation."

"You don't have any leads, do you?"

"Not yet, but you'll be the first one I call if I do." It was technically the truth. The blackmail note wasn't a lead...yet. "Thanks again."

"Welcome. Agnes, we'll see you tomorrow morning, first thing."

Before I could disconnect, Agnes laughed. "As long as *first thing* means *after noon.*"

"Thanks again, officer." This time I managed to end the call before anything else was said.

Grabbing the pen again, I made another note detailing what he'd shared about the murder weapon. "So far we know that neither Agnes nor her highly coveted dining room table is guilty of this crime. Let's focus on the note again. We're agreed that the dollar amount suggests that it's not solely the money the perp is after since if that was the case, they would've asked for a whole lot more."

Agnes giggled. "Perp?"

I sighed. It was going to be a long night. I rolled my eyes and offered Tan a small smile. I was glad he was here with me. "What would you like to call him or her?"

"Charlie," Agnes offered without hesitation.

This time Tan chuckled. "Any particular reason?"

Agnes half walked, half stumbled over to the table. She picked up the blackmailer's note. "Isn't that what they called the bad guys in the Vietnam War? My marriage to Rico reminds me of a war zone. It feels appropriate."

Tanner nodded. "Charlie it is then."

Agnes returned to her seat and poured more of the tequila in her glass. She sipped it slowly, which I took as a good sign. "So other than being a nice round number, why a quarter of a million dollars?"

"Maybe he doesn't want to be too greedy," Tan offered as an explanation right before his stomach growled. "You got anything to eat, Agnes? I'm starving."

She nodded. "I have some food Chef Jonathan brought by earlier today. Since I wasn't home, he left it with my neighbors. Let me get it for you."

"Have you eaten any of it yet, Agnes?" I had to know if her meal tasted as bad as the one I'd been forced to endure.

"No, all of this nonsense has given me no appetite. Plus, I'm still not one hundred percent recovered from my queasy stomach. I had some of the tea from Rico when I first got home, but that didn't calm me enough—just left me feeling ill. I switched to my tequila." Agnes stood and moved toward the kitchen. "Let me heat a plate for you. You want anything, Lilly?"

I'd rather starve than eat one more bite of Chef Jonathan's cooking. "Could I have some of your tea? It doesn't have to be the one Rico gave you if you'd like to hold on to it for sentimental reasons."

Bitter laughter filled the large room. "That bast— backstabbing man..." She looked at me and winked. Agnes continued, "No wonder she won't move in with you, Tanner. She won't even curse. You've gone and got yourself *too* good of a girl."

I ignored Agnes's comment and managed to keep from sharing my reasoning. Agnes probably wouldn't care that Gram had been the one against cursing. It was out of respect for her, not some sense of being high and mighty, that I curbed the cursing. Not wanting to dwell on my lack of cursing or my living arrangements, I urged Agnes to continue. "Go on"

"That man lied to me, stole from me, and is still managing to make my life difficult even in death. You really think I want to hold on to some tea leaves he gave me? Probably used *my* money to buy it for me."

The woman had a point. "Touché. Then let's make it a really big mug of steaming Rico-Cheating Tea."

My comment earned me heartfelt chuckles from both of my companions. I'd take that. I felt a little guilty about not warning Tanner about the food, but he was hungry. Maybe if Agnes saw his reaction, she'd realize investing in the restaurant wasn't such a good idea.

A few minutes later, I had my tea, Tanner had his dinner, and Agnes had switched to water with lemon. Maybe she was starting to see the trouble tequila could bring, especially given she had to make a statement to the police tomorrow.

Tanner scarfed down the food without so much as a wrinkle of his nose. I, on the other hand, thought the tea tasted nasty. Maybe it was *my* taste buds that were in the wrong here. "How's your dinner, Tan?"

He looked up from his plate long enough to smile one of those forget-my-name smiles. Seriously, what was I going to do if he left? Besides remember my name, that was.

"It's delicious. You sure you don't want some?"

I shook my head and turned to Agnes. "Did this tea taste funny to you?"

She shrugged as she continued to look through an album she'd made of pictures from her cruise. The tortured look on her face reminded me that at least for a moment in time, she'd loved Rico.

"I didn't notice, but you're asking a woman who drinks tequila straight up without even flinching."

Score another point for Agnes. "Fair enough. Maybe it's just me." I cast another glance at Tanner, still happily eating some steak-and-vegetable entrée. Dutifully, I returned to my notepaper and the tea. "Did you find anything of interest when you went through his things? Something that would explain the envelope of cash?"

Tanner managed to drag his adorable, sauce-covered face away from his dinner. "What envelope of cash?"

Oh, right. I hadn't filled him in on all of that. It wasn't like the lines of communication had been transferring data at broadband speeds between us lately. "When I was helping Agnes by looking for her ring—"

"Fake ring," she interjected.

"Right. When I was helping Agnes by looking for her *fake* ring, I found an envelope of cash under the hutch over there." I pointed to the opposite side of the room.

"How much was in it?" Tanner asked.

"Ten thousand dollars," Agnes supplied with a sigh.

"Interesting—another nice round number. How come no one ever asks for $9,782 or something like that?"

"Don't forget the seventy-two cents," I teased. His query made me think though. "Maybe Rico was being blackmailed too."

"Do you think it's the same person?" Agnes pushed the album aside and focused on our conversation.

I shrugged. "I can't be sure, but why ask for ten grand from Rico and a quarter of a million from you? If what you see on television is based in any truth, there's usually a reason for the specific amount the blackmailer asks for."

"Rounded to the nearest thousand." Tanner moved his plate aside. "Maybe the blackmailer worried Rico wouldn't be able to get his hands on that much money without raising Agnes's attention."

"Makes sense, but where's the note? Agnes, did you find anything that could be construed as a blackmail note?"

She shook her head. "Nothing personal at all really. Just some receipts from places he visited around here. Veggie Tables, The Pelican Bar, and of course the bank, but no official receipts for those withdrawals."

I leaned back in the chair and closed my eyes. There was something about the number that was eluding me. Something that would make sense. Slowly, I walked my mind through the past few days to identify everyone I could think of that Rico had come in contact with. Of course the list wouldn't be comprehensive as I hadn't been with him every moment, but a girl had to start somewhere. I remembered the argument between Rico and Jonathan the day of the brunch.

"Since we can't find a note, maybe we're thinking about this all wrong. Maybe Rico was blackmailing someone? Maybe he or she stopped by to make the payment, things got out of hand, and bam, Rico's dead."

Tanner sat forward in his chair. I took that as a sign he thought the theory was at least plausible. "If he had access to all of Agnes's money, why would he need to blackmail someone?"

Good question. There was a reason it was a theory. "I'm not sure."

"He didn't have access to all of my money," Agnes explained. "He only had access to one account, which has a reasonable balance in it, but I also had alerts on the account so I could monitor his activity."

"Didn't you say Rico had withdrawn ten grand though?" If I'd remembered that a few minutes ago, my theory about him being the blackmailer wouldn't have even been shared with the rest of the class.

"Wait!" Agnes stood and went to the printer sitting on the desk in her living room. A moment later, she returned with a printout. "I'd almost forgotten about this. In addition to looking through paperwork, I checked his web browser. His search engine revealed he'd been looking at these jeans."

Tanner's eyes bulged when he saw the picture and the price tag. "Ten thousand for a pair of jeans! Seriously? I had some designer clothes back when my dad was alive, but never anything like this. Are those real diamonds on the back pockets?"

"Yes, they are. I assume he put the charge on his personal credit card and planned on using the cash to pay off the balance. I won't know for sure until his statement arrives though."

Okay, so my theory might be plausible. I decided to toss out one more wild and crazy idea. "If we go back to our original idea that Rico was the one being blackmailed, do you think Jonathan might be the one blackmailing him?"

Agnes's eyes widened. "What possible reason would he have for doing that?"

I chewed on my bottom lip for a few moments before answering. "I saw them arguing after the brunch. Rico threatened Jonathan, telling him he'd never get a dime of your money, but then Jonathan made a comment about starting to understand how personal this was for Rico. If it was just about the money, what else would there be to understand? Maybe Jonathan knew a secret about Rico—something that would jeopardize his relationship with Agnes. Or maybe it has something to do with Allyson. I'm convinced the three of them have history together."

"We can assume Rico and Allyson had a history given their interaction at the brunch. And based on her statements that day, we know Allyson and Jonathan dated previously." Tanner confirmed at least two-thirds of my statement, or would that be three-fourths? "Maybe they ran in the same social circle?"

Agnes plopped into the chair. "Anything's possible, and none of it makes much sense to me right now."

And any arrangement they had was null and void now that Rico was dead. "You're right, Agnes. Anything's possible."

She yawned. "I'm too tired to think about it anymore tonight. I have to give a statement to the police in the morning. I need to be at my best so I don't get arrested."

I stood and gathered the notes I'd written and slipped them into my purse. "Bottom line is that we need more proof before we can share anything with the police anyway."

Agnes nodded before walking from the dining room into her living room. The plush leather recliner swallowed her frame, sending stray cat hairs floating onto the floor. As though her sitting offered an invitation, both of her cats jumped up into her lap, offering the feline version of comforting. "What I need right now is a plan. Between the blackmail note and the police interview tomorrow, I'm not sure what to do."

Right. We needed a plan. "You get a good night's rest. Make sure you have an attorney present. Attorney Pohoke is my recommendation. He's gotten me out of trouble more times than I care to admit. He's very good at his job."

"If you could find the blackmail note the perp..." Tanner turned to me and smiled. "Might have given to Rico, that would be helpful. It would set up an alternative theory to his murder."

Agnes slid her hands under both cats and snuggled them close. I think the purring brought her comfort.

"Alternative to me being the murderer, you mean."

Tanner looked like a deer caught in the halogen headlights of an oncoming Jeep. Yeah, he wasn't used to dealing with suspects, perps, and the like. His job was to swoop in at the last minute and rescue me. I stepped between him and Agnes. "All Tanner is *trying* to do is keep you out of Detective Marshall's line of fire."

"Should I tell them about the blackmail note I received?"

"Yes." "No." Tanner and I answered simultaneously.

"Lilly, she needs to tell the truth."

He clearly hadn't been interrogated as many times as I had. In retrospect, that probably wasn't a bad thing. "I'm not suggesting she lie. You know how I feel about that. I just want her to hold off until we have more she can tell the police."

Agnes moved the cats to the arm of her chair. They were not pleased, if the look they gave her was any indication. She pacified them with scratching under the chin, and all seemed to be forgiven. Too bad it didn't work that way with humans. "What do you want me to do, Lilly?"

"I want you to go through with it. Pay the ransom."

CHAPTER SEVENTEEN

———

Somehow I'd managed to convince Tanner to wait for me outside while I went over the details of my crazy plan with Agnes. After some debate and given my history with the police, we decided Agnes would take a copy of the blackmail note to them and suggest a sting operation to catch the bad guy. It mirrored my original plan, just with Agnes doing the convincing rather than me. I really hoped she'd be able to convince them to establish a perimeter to watch the drop site and move in when the perp—yeah, that word was definitely growing on me— moved in to claim the money. I remembered now why I didn't normally include Tan in this part of my investigations. Mandi was normally my accomplice. She was up for a little more adventure than my knight in white cotton. He would save us from our zany plan when things went wrong…which they always did. I reasoned that meant I was long overdue for one to go right. Not that I'd participated in a lot of investigations, two up to this point to be exact. Not a single one of them official, but I'd managed to help the police—despite what they thought— catch the bad guy both times.

Agnes had sent me home with a box of tea, a different variety from what she'd been drinking since I hadn't cared for the taste. She absently informed me that this had been a gift from Rico as well. Guess she really didn't mind parting with any past tokens of his alleged affection. She'd insisted on it as a way to thank me for my help. This blend was decaf and supposed to help me sleep. I'd accepted, if for no other reason than to get out of the house.

Of course, Tan was waiting to share with me his thoughts on the plan. "You've lost your mind."

"Hear me out. Whoever is blackmailing Agnes either knows enough about her history with Rico, along with what happened that afternoon, to believe he or she can convince the police she meant to kill her husband or..."

"Or what?" Tan demanded.

"Or that person is the killer."

"And you still think it's a good idea to invite this person into your backyard?"

The incredulous inflection in his question indicated he not only thought it wasn't a good idea, he thought my idea stunk to high heaven.

"You were right about one thing. Agnes is going to tell them about the note, and she'll do the convincing. At least that's the plan."

He shook his head. Couldn't say that I blamed him. "It's crazy. I know. It's just a gut feeling I have that this is what we need to do to fix all of this."

We slid into the front seat of the Mustang. Nice plush leather, minus the cat hair. I laid my head back waiting for the lecture I figured he was going to give me. Instead, the warmth of his lips touched my cheek. I turned to face him, certain I was dreaming. The glow from the dash lights heightened his angular jaw and made me forget all about blackmail and murder for a moment. The next time he learned forward was to bestow the same gentle kiss on my lips.

Warmth circulated throughout my body, a gentle rain shower of emotion slowly washing away the dirt and grime of the past few days. This. This was how it was supposed to be. Tan pulled away only enough to speak. I could feel the curve of his smile against my lips.

"I may not always agree with your methods, but you've proven that they work."

Tears threatened at the sweet words he spoke. Always before we'd end up fighting about what he believed were unnecessary risks I took from time to time. Had this change of heart come about because we'd grown and matured? Or was it because he knew he was leaving and didn't want to spend the last bit of our time together fighting a useless fight? He knew I wasn't going to change—at least not a three-sixty turnaround. I decided to play nice in the sandbox too. "Thank you, Tan. That means a lot."

"I'm here for you. Now should I take you home so that you can get some rest before the big day tomorrow?"

This would be a big test of the newfound faith in me he'd just expressed. "Actually, would you mind taking me to Ocean View first?"

He started the car, a low rumble that vibrated throughout my entire core. Goodness, I loved that feeling. Made a girl feel alive!

"It's really late, Lilly. After midnight. I don't think anyone will be up."

I pulled out my phone and texted Bree. *You awake?*

Less than thirty seconds later, she replied. *Yep. What's up?*

Has Allyson returned?
She's sitting alone on the glider on the back porch.
Okay if I pay her a visit?
*Free country *grin**
Thx. See you soon.

I held the phone up to Tan to prove it was okay to stop by. "You can go home if you're tired after you drop me off. Ocean View isn't far from the tavern. I can get my bike and go home from there."

He pulled out onto Cliffside Drive, one of the main roads that ran through Danger Cove, and headed in the direction of the B&B. "Just because I'm trying to be supportive of your reckless behavior doesn't mean I'm going to let you go all Wild West on your own."

Now there was the man I'd come to…Was it the *L* word? Years of promising myself I wouldn't fall in love taunted me. I couldn't deny that I felt stronger about Tan than I had any other guy that I'd spent time with in the past, yet love struck an all-in chord that I wasn't sure I was ready to play. Ugh, this was all such a mess. Although I couldn't tell him yet, I could admit it to myself: Even if I hadn't officially fallen in love, I was definitely slipping in that direction. I opted for something much lighter yet still conveyed a little of the emotional hold he'd managed to secure me in. I grabbed his hand and squeezed. "The Wild West is more fun when you're there with me anyway. Thanks."

The warm night made it perfect for rolling the windows down. The breeze tossed my hair in disarray and cooled my skin. The moment was carefree and the silence companionable. I really did want to take a long drive with Tan someday. It didn't even matter where. Just the two of us, the open road, and the gentle breeze. Yeah, that would be nice.

Finally, Tanner spoke. "You don't really think Chef Jonathan was the one to blackmail Rico, do you?"

"I don't know for sure, and to be honest, the timing of everything doesn't really work out. He's the most probable suspect though. I witnessed Rico threatening Jonathan after the brunch. He told him he wasn't going to get a dime of Agnes's money."

I turned to face him. "Mentioning the brunch reminds me. Did you really like the food you ate at Agnes's tonight?"

He shrugged. "It wasn't the best, but filled the hole. Tasted a little off to me, but I've had worse. It was better than some of the meals Ashley has whipped up in the past couple years."

"Good to know. For the unofficial record, I won't be letting your little sister near the food, even if Tara does bail and take Chef Jonathan up on his offer. For the official record, you're entirely too good of a faker. I thought you really liked the food."

"I was starving! I'd barely eaten all day. It went down so fast, I could barely taste it. A detail for which I was very grateful."

"That's good to know should I ever cook you a meal."

This time his laughter bubbled all the way up and out of his body. "If you ever cooked me a meal, I would eat it with slow deliberation, savoring every bite, as it would certainly be my last."

Not cool. Not cool at all. "Tanner Montgomery! That's not very nice. Are you saying my cooking would kill you?"

We pulled into the parking lot at Ocean View, which allowed him to put the car in park and turn to face me. "Not at all. I only meant that if you actually cooked a meal, there could be no other explanation than the world was ending."

In reply to his snarky comment, he received a punch in the arm, and I stuck my tongue out at him. "Very funny, pretty boy. For that little confession, you can wait here while I talk to Allyson."

"Just Allyson, right?"

I nodded. "Just Allyson, promise."

The Ocean View Bed & Breakfast was a beautiful home with a porch that wrapped all the way around the structure. I'd spent a fair amount of time sitting on both the front and back porch. It was easy to see why Bree was so successful in running the place, even though she couldn't cook any better than me. The breakfast part of the bed and breakfast was essentially catered by the Cinnamon Sugar Bakery in town, which no one had ever complained about. There was a feeling she somehow managed to generate each time someone stepped onto the property. From the colors of the paint, to the comfy chairs on the porch, and finally to the warm hospitality she gave every guest, it was easy to see why people were happy to call Ocean View home for whatever time they stayed.

Maybe everyone was right and it was time for me to find a place I could call home. It was also possible that Tan's kisses had made me wax all sentimental and I wasn't thinking clearly. Truly hard to tell when under the influence of warm fuzzies.

Using the flashlight app on my phone, I made my way around to the back. Just as Bree indicated, Allyson was sitting on the glider, slowly moving back and forth. The sound of the waves crashing in the distance engendered a sense of calm to anyone who took the time to hear the steady rhythms. "Peaceful, isn't it?"

"Mmmm, very much so. San Francisco is much busier, noisier. Hard to hear the whispers of the waves."

Maybe she wasn't a complete witch. She understood the dichotomy of the power and peace of the ocean. "Okay if I sit?"

"Of course. What can I do for you, Lilly?" She stared off into the distance.

Though her words had been polite, she'd yet to look in my direction. It was dark—maybe she felt eye contact was unnecessary.

"I'm working on a theory. I think Rico was being blackmailed prior to his death."

Because of the distinct lack of lighting, I could see no outward reaction to my statement, but I could feel one. Tension seeped into her body like a coiling snake. I needed to tread lightly to avoid a potential bite.

After several seconds, she replied, "And?"

"And do you think Chef Jonathan had a motive for blackmailing Rico?" I wanted to mention Agnes but still couldn't figure any plausible motive, since she'd already indicated her intent to invest.

My question earned a heartfelt chuckle from Allyson. I hadn't meant the inquiry to be amusing, but I guess each person had different pressure points for the funny bone.

"Does Jonathan look like a blackmailer to you?"

"Ummm, well, to be honest, I didn't realize there were physical requirements to fit into that category of criminal." At that moment, I preferred the peace of the crashing waves to her judgmental tone.

She turned to look at me—finally. Even in the dim light, I could see loss in her eyes rather than laughter. "It's not so much a physical appearance, but a presence they have. They are smooth, often sexy, and have a driving desire to find the weaknesses in others and exploit them. If Jonathan were a blackmailer, he would have approached you privately and threatened to go to the tabloids or any interested newspaper about the sordid details of your personal life unless you gave him the money he wanted."

I didn't like the direction this conversation had taken. I preferred offense as opposed to defense in these situations. "What do you mean, sordid details?"

Allyson waved her hand as if the *sordid* details of my life—whatever they might be—were insignificant. "Oh, please, mommy runs off with rebel rocker, gets pregnant, drops baby at grandmother's doorstep, and never looks back. That is until twenty some years later…"

I stood up and started to pace. "You made your point. You can stop now."

"My point is, Lilly, he didn't do that. He approached you in a very public place and shared an opportunity for you to consider. That is not how a blackmailer operates."

After pacing the length of the porch a few more times for emphasis, I returned to my seat next to her. "You sure know a lot about this particular kind of crime and the people that perpetrate them. Anything you want to share? Personal experience maybe?" It was true. My nose had a problem. It stuck itself into other people's business—despite not liking others sticking their nose into mine. The double standard lived loud and proud in this area of my life, I admit. Not something I was particularly proud of, but the truth.

"You want to know what a blackmailer looks like? Take a good, long look at Agnes's wedding photos. Her husband was among the best."

"Rico?" I'd pegged him for a money-grubbing con artist, but the blackmailer theory was really just a shot-in-the-dark guess. I hadn't held much conviction for that theory. "Why would he blackmail Agnes? He had access, for the most part, to her fortune." There were limits, I'd learned, but still...

She turned to stare back into the distance and initiate the gentle rocking motion of the glider again. "He didn't blackmail Agnes—at least not that I'm aware of. He blackmailed me."

CHAPTER EIGHTEEN

———

Her word bomb exploded on me, destroying every preconceived notion I'd developed about her in one decisive burst. "I don't suppose you'd care to elaborate?" It was a long shot, but one I felt compelled to take.

"I don't suppose it matters now anyway. He's dead, and I have Jonathan back."

Her explanation was sounding more and more like motive for murder to me, but I decided to keep quiet—for once—and let her continue. I didn't have to wait long.

"I'm sure you saw in the tabloids that Jonathan left me because I cheated on him."

"I heard."

"What the tabloids didn't mention is that it wasn't like Jonathan discovered me in bed with another man. I *told* him about the affair."

"So you did cheat."

"I did. Remember our conversation from the other day when I told you that sometimes things are so good that we sabotage them ourselves before nature takes its course?"

How could I forget? She'd shed some unwanted insight on my situation with Tan. "I remember."

"Things were so beautiful between Jonathan and me I couldn't believe my luck. He was smart, successful, sexy, and the man could cook. He took an interest in me—a nobody from the suburbs of Seattle."

It never ceased to amaze me how negatively we, as women, viewed ourselves. We truly were our own worst critics. "It's not like you don't have anything to offer. You're smart, beautiful, and possess a fierce determination." She'd certainly come across fierce that morning at Charlie's.

She patted my leg. "That's sweet of you to say, Lilly. You don't understand how the rules change the higher up the power ladder you climb."

She was right. I didn't. Other than bucking for a promotion at Smugglers' Tavern, and that was more financial than power related, I'd been content to sit on whatever power rung that life guided me to rest. No climbing necessary. "Since I'm a bartender, the struggle for power hasn't been something I've had to contend with. I'm sure the higher the stakes, the heavier the hammer that gets dropped on you."

Allyson let her head drop back as though the weight of her confession was more than she could bear. "You're right. Jonathan wasn't just climbing—he was taking an elevator to the top. People were either jealous of him or they wanted to be him. Constant whispers in his direction about what he should be doing or who he could trust. While I was happy for him, I missed there being time for the two of us to relax together, just to be. Does that make sense?"

I thought about all the times Tan and I would go for a walk or grab an ice cream cone and sit on the end of the pier, our feet dangling over the edge. Not a care in the world. Just him and me. "It does."

"Rico came along and gave me the one thing Jonathan wasn't giving me at the time—attention."

"Did you try to talk to Jonathan? Share with him how much you missed him?" I felt like Tan and I had at least kept a somewhat open line of communication, even if the busy signal did create interference from time to time.

She shook her head. "Not as hard as I should have. He was focused on his career. People were clamoring for his time and attention. I couldn't, didn't, compete."

"But Rico listened."

"Oh, he listened and talked—said all the right things. See, that's the thing about blackmailers and con artists. They know just what you want to hear and feed it to you with the sweetest of spoons. I ate it up like a starving infant. By the time I realized what he was up to, it was too late."

The waves crashed three or four times before I felt compelled to fill the silence. "He threatened to tell Jonathan if you didn't pay?"

"Ten thousand dollars." The bitterness of her voice crackled in the night air. "I don't know why he thought I had access to that kind of money."

The irony that there was ten thousand dollars in the envelope I found at Agnes's house wasn't lost on me. Of course, I still didn't know if Rico was being blackmailed or if he *was* the blackmailer. Now that I knew Allyson had been blackmailed, maybe she'd tried to turn the tables on Rico as payback for ruining her relationship with Jonathan. Though what sordid details about Rico's life she might possess, I couldn't be sure. "You dress like you have money. Maybe that, along with being Jonathan's girlfriend, made him think you were rolling in the dough? He might have thought you were higher up the ladder than you really were."

"Whatever his thought process, it was wrong. I have an aunt who designs clothes for a boutique in Los Angeles. The label isn't as posh or recognizable as some of the bigger designers, but the clothes are stylish and well made. I happen to be her favorite niece, and my size and body shape fit nicely into her designs. She keeps me in style. I provide word of mouth advertising."

My guess was there weren't too many labels Allyson wouldn't look good in, but she was sharing important details. I'd save the compliments for later. "That's a sweet deal. I guess that's why Rico must've thought you had cash flow. Designer labels, even the less recognizable ones, come with a nice price tag." If it turned out she wasn't the blackmailer, maybe I'd allocate some of my inheritance to updating my closet with clothes from…"What's the name of the designer? You know…just in case I'm in the area." Or on the website.

Allyson lifted her head and turned to look at me, a small smile on her face. "VV, which stands for Vivian Victor. She does some vintage pieces that I think you'd like. Remind me tomorrow, and I'll give you her card."

"That's great, thank you. But back on topic. So Rico asked for ten grand—you didn't have it. Did you try to borrow the money, either from the bank or a family member?" I was thinking Aunt Vivian could've parted with the cash easily to keep her niece out of the tabloids. Then again, maybe her designs on the front page of even a sketchy magazine would be good for business? That might be one of those too-high-on-the-power-ladder ploys for publicity for me to understand.

"I thought about it briefly, but decided I'd created the mess, and no one should clean it up but me."

She was still hanging around on my suspect list, but I had to admit my respect for the woman had climbed a rung or two since our conversation had started. "You told Jonathan yourself and removed the threat of blackmail."

"Yes, I did. Of course, some of the women who were waiting in the wings for a chance to attach themselves to him and his status found out."

"And they shared the story with the tabloids. No one knew it was Rico though. You didn't tell Jonathan who it was…only that there was someone else."

"Right. Who I'd had the affair with wasn't important, especially because I didn't love him and certainly didn't want to be with him anymore after the blackmail threat. The only thing Jonathan needed to know was that I *had* an affair."

"That took guts and class."

Allyson smiled. "I suppose that's one way of looking at it. Thanks for seeing the best in me. Not too many people have, especially after the tabloids were through."

"But Jonathan and you are back together. He obviously saw the good in you too."

The smile faded. "Something like that." She stood. "It's getting late. I should be turning in. Big day tomorrow. Good night, Lilly."

I stood to follow her. Why did I feel like I'd taken two steps forward and three and a half steps back on the information trail? "Allyson, wait."

She stopped but didn't turn around. "I'm really tired. No more talking tonight, okay?"

It wasn't okay. I suppose I could've followed her into the house, but there didn't seem to be any point. She'd been forthcoming with so many details. But then when I brought up a detail she'd mentioned earlier—she and Jonathan being back together—something changed. It didn't make any sense.

"Everything okay?" Tanner's deep, soft voice filtered in from the corner of the house.

I turned toward him and crossed my arms, but my smile softened the effect, even if he couldn't see me clearly. "Exactly how long have you been spying on me, Mr. Montgomery?"

He took the steps necessary to join me and guided us to the glider. His arm went around my shoulders, and I didn't resist. Who knew how many more moments like this we might have. "I've been hanging around the corner for the last ten or fifteen minutes. I didn't want to interrupt, but wanted to make sure you were okay."

"You wanted to make sure I was only speaking with Allyson," I teased.

A chuckle reverberated through his muscular chest. "Maybe that too."

It would've been the most natural thing in the world right then to tell him I was slipping into love with him, but lifelong habits weren't easily undone. Also, I didn't want him to feel like I was saying it to unduly influence his decision on whether or not to take the job in Chicago. "Since you heard everything, why do you think she clammed up at the end? I only reiterated what she'd shared in the beginning. Thought that was Interrogation 101—start with where you agree."

Tanner laughed and pulled me closer. "I think that's Negotiation 101."

"Oh…well, it sounded good."

"I was thinking about it while you two were talking," Tan started.

My head was nestled against his shoulder, allowing the calm pitch of his voice to soothe my confused nerves. "And? Any big revelations I should know about?"

"She kept referring to his status being higher than hers. The pressure to keep his status had him focus on things other than her. He had the status. She didn't."

He was right. That was a common theme throughout her story. "But nothing changed. He's still the chef at the top of his game. He's opening a new restaurant, seeking investors, and taking things to the next level. I'll add that includes trying to poach *my* chef."

Tanner laughed. "I like how you refer to her as yours. You're taking managing the tavern and the responsibility Hope gave you very seriously. It kind of turns me on."

I twisted in his embrace and gave him a quick kiss. "Like it takes much to turn you on."

"No argument there. And you're right. Nothing changed as far as we know in the dynamic between Allyson and Jonathan, but what if it had?"

Something Mandi had said earlier marched itself to the forefront of my brain. "Like what if Chef Jonathan had lost his ability to taste?"

We glided back and forth a few times—at least four wave crashes—before Tan spoke. "That would explain the less-than-perfect food."

I sat up straight, information initiating a rapid-fire, high-powered weapon in the synapses of my brain. "He must have somehow found out about Agnes's big lottery win, so he came here looking for a big investor."

Tan nodded. "If he looked up Agnes on the internet, he probably found out about you, as you were mentioned in the same article with her."

"Right. He might also have assumed that we were outside of the circle of influence of the five-star restaurants in the big cities. Even if we'd heard of him, chances are we wouldn't know all the details about him. If it hadn't been for Tara telling me about him and the *Haute Cuisine* magazine, I wouldn't have even known he existed."

"Allyson mentioned there were always people waiting in the wings, acting on any information they might be privy to. What if someone close to him, a sous chef maybe, realized what was happening? Sounds like a good way to move up another rung on the power ladder and become head chef." Tanner's voice had grown animated as he put possible pieces together.

We could both be way off base, but just playing in the same field was fun.

"Jonathan decides to be proactive, and opportunity presented itself when he learned of the millions just waiting here for him in Danger Cove."

"Don't forget to add that Allyson has to know his secret. She ate his food the other night. No way could she have done so and not realized he'd lost his golden touch."

Tanner pulled me close, his lips a breath away. "Equals a shift in the relationship."

My lips tingled from his closeness, making it hard to say anything further. When the man was right, he was right. Being right, in this moment, deserved a reward. "Who should take the power here and initiate this kiss?"

His fingers slid up my cheek and into my hair. "As long as you kiss me, I don't care."

We both moved at the same time. Equal power. I liked that. My eyes closed at the touch of his lips against mine.

"If you two need a room, I'll have to charge you a fifty-dollar deposit. Cash or credit."

CHAPTER NINETEEN

———

After Bree managed to ruin a memorable Hallmark moment in the making, Tanner and I excused ourselves. I could hear her laughter following us as we made our way around the house. I was sure I'd hear more from her on the matter later. For now, I was excited that we at least might have gained a little deeper understanding of Jonathan and his motive for coming to Danger Cove.

Did he have motives for other events that had taken place since his arrival? That was still to be determined. Despite Tan driving like a ninety-year-old man on the way home, we still pulled into the lot at Hazlitt Heights entirely too fast. I slid across the seat and snuggled in for a few more minutes of quality time, despite the late hour.

"You want me to come up and brainstorm some more with you?" Tanner's words were muffled due to his mouth being buried in my tangled hair.

All my girly parts screamed a silent *Yes!* But they weren't fooling me at all. Their reasons for wanting him to come up had nothing to do with our brains, at least not directly. They had a valid argument though. Tan could be leaving. Shouldn't we—what was the expression? Leave it all on the field. Donna Do-Good, the name I'd given to my responsible angel, reminded me that inviting Tan up for anything more than the aforementioned brainstorming could unfairly influence his decision about the Chicago job. I didn't want to be *that* girl. Keep the power even—that was the goal.

Instead, I kissed him with purpose, intent on conveying what words were inadequate for at this crossroads in our relationship. "We should get some rest. Tomorrow is a long day, and we both need to be sharp. Thank you for—well, everything tonight."

His fingers slid from my cheek, the light touch and his smile warming my already heated heart. "We get through tomorrow and then we talk about us and the future."

I opened my mouth to say that we'd already outlined our positions. The decision rested with him. Of course, that meant I was totally ignoring decisions I had to make. Double standard alive and well. Before I could give lip to my litany, his index finger pressed against my mouth, rendering me silent.

"Good night, Lilly. Sweet and sexy dreams."

The last part was added with one of his saucy smiles, making me reevaluate if I should give Ms. Do-Good the night off. One quick kiss later, I replied, "Good night, Tanner."

My bedtime routine took longer than normal as my brain was preoccupied from all I'd learned in the past twelve hours or so. Was I making the right decision about Agnes and the blackmailer? Putting myself in danger was one thing—bringing Agnes into the mix was another matter entirely.

Not wanting to get into a circular moral debate with myself, I put in the CD my parents had sent and hoped the music would lull me to sleep. It was almost two in the morning, which meant the alarm would be going off in a little over five hours. We didn't open until ten, but I liked to get in early and deal with any necessary paperwork before the team arrived around nine to prep for the day.

The melody did its best to lure my mind into the murky depths of blissful rest. Unanswered questions kept striking an offbeat rhythm into the tune, preventing the solace of sleep. Finally, I grabbed my notepad from the table next to the bed and wrote down the questions depriving me of my shut-eye:

Was someone blackmailing Rico and why?
Why was Agnes being blackmailed for $250,000?
What happened to Agnes's (fake) ring?
What would I do if Tanner took the job in Chicago?

I was sure there were more questions I needed to write down, but the boulder in my stomach at the final one I'd penned took away my will to ask any more. Since I couldn't rest, I decided to try the tea that Agnes had given me earlier tonight. I sat at the table with my notebook and took my first tentative sip of the new tea. This one was much nicer than the last—a hint of orange and something else I couldn't place. That happened with more regularity these days. Maybe I should take a cooking class or something. Ha! In my spare time? I usually slept during my few free hours.

Once half of the cup of tea was gone, I refocused on the first question. Who would blackmail Rico? Allyson would be the logical choice, but given the distaste she'd had for when it was done to her, I couldn't see her turning the tables, especially given the fact that she'd not actually paid the blackmail.

Jonathan was a possibility, but I still couldn't think of a reason or what secret of Rico's he might be aware of that would translate into his being paid to keep silent. Agnes was the only other person I could think of, and that made no sense. She would know he could simply get the money from her account to pay—which was exactly what he did. Unless she was doing it to test him? If Agnes already started to suspect Rico was in it for the money, that could've been a ten-thousand-dollar test. Enough to get his attention, but small enough that he could get access to the funds.

Before continuing my line of thought on Agnes, I took a small detour to the subject of the missing ring. Both Agnes and I, along with the police, had searched her home. The police had searched tavern property, along with my home, and the ring hadn't turned up. Did that mean Agnes's would-be blackmailer had the ring? It was also logical to assume the blackmailer and killer were one and the same person. Wasn't it? Or, I sighed, maybe not.

Returning my thoughts to Agnes, what an interesting development it would be if she were the one behind all of this. Here I had been worried I might need to run an intervention for Agnes. Instead, she might have moved up a few rungs on the cunning-and-evil ladder. I had to be honest and admit to myself that this wasn't the first time I'd considered the possibility that Agnes had been taking advantage of me and our friendship throughout this whole ordeal.

The blackmail note for the quarter of a mil had appeared to take her by surprise. If this newest blackmail was part of her elaborate plot, she'd performed on an Academy Award level. Agnes had always been a what-you-see-is-what-you-get kind of gal, so I was leaning toward the notion that this development was something not even she had anticipated. I was on the merry-go-round of reasoning, and the ride was making me nauseous. Literally.

I set the tea aside, unsure if it wasn't agreeing with me or if this nightmare of the past few days was setting my tummy in turmoil. Back to my list of questions. Not like I'd made *any* progress on it, but I couldn't sleep, so might as well keep at it.

The only other person I could think of was not a strong candidate. Steven Sinclair. I simply didn't know him well enough to know whether he had a motive or not. As Jonathan's business partner and close friend to Allyson, there was logic in thinking he might have tried to blackmail Rico to make sure he'd not stand in Agnes's way and to get some retribution for Allyson. Clara had mentioned that Allyson and Steven were "intense." Maybe Steven's actions could have been motivated by chivalry and loyalty?

There was also the issue of the murder weapon. With only knowing it was a blunt item that packed a punch and didn't leave any table residue in the wound, I didn't have much to go on. There were any number of items in Agnes's house that she would have had access to. Though not in my kitchen, I remembered Gram having a rolling pin that I was sure could've created enough impact to do some damage.

If Allyson had been the killer, she could've used a weapon of opportunity—something in Agnes's house or something brought with her. Same with Steven. Images of Steven and his fashion accessory flashed in my brain. Could Steven's walking stick have inflicted a mortal blow to Rico's skull? I wasn't sure what material it was made from, but it looked sturdy. I put my head down on the table. This felt like an exercise in futility. Not only were there multiple suspects, but a thousand different potential weapons. Those had to be worse odds than Vegas.

With no blackmail note to explain the ten thousand dollars, there was no way to tell. This detail annoyed me. If it weren't the middle of the night, I would have texted Mandi to ask for statistics on how many blackmails were carried out that weren't accompanied by a note.

The timing for everything just felt…off. I hated when that happened—usually meant I was overlooking some important detail. My eyelashes were putting on weight, making it difficult for me to keep my eyes open. My brain, on the other hand, was a beehive of activity. Giving in to the fatigue, I decided I could still allow my brain to do its thing with my eyes closed. The only two remaining questions—not that I'd answered a single one on the list yet—was the amount on the blackmail note and my distress over the situation with Tanner.

Yeah, let's focus on the blackmail demand. Easier and less emotional for me. I searched the archive of my mind to try to remember exactly how much Agnes had won in the lottery. It was possible blackmailer had arrived at the number as a percentage of the winnings.

I'd need a calculator for this, as I knew Agnes had won in the tens of millions of dollars. If the blackmailer knew that and only asked for two hundred and fifty thousand, they should have their criminal card revoked. Seriously! Any bad guy worth their salt would have at least asked for an even million. They would have to know that Agnes could pay that without blinking an eye. A quarter of that was like making a withdrawal from petty cash for her.

No. It had to be something else.

Maybe it had to do with Agnes's life before she became filthy rich. She'd worked as a dispatcher and front desk administrator at the local police department. Maybe she'd denied someone access to visiting a loved one because they didn't possess the proper identification and they were out for revenge? She'd almost done the same to me once, but her softer side had prevailed, and she'd let me visit my mom with only a library card and debit card to prove my identity.

I pounded the pillow a few times for good measure. This was getting me nowhere. I decided to focus on Tanner. Not on the fact that he might be leaving, but rather on all the happy times we'd had. Yeah, that could lead to sweet dreams. At least a few thousand worth, right?

The alarm sounded before I could finish even one sweet dream. I hit the snooze button and decided to let the dream play out before I started my day. Tan and I had gone to Seattle on one of our days off. This was before I had full access to my inheritance, so neither of us had much money. We'd used the majority of what we had to gain access to the top of the Space Needle. Tanner had held my hand as we took in the sight of Mount Rainier in all its breathtaking beauty. The snow-capped mountain stood proudly against the clear sky, almost daring the city to try to conquer the over-fourteen-thousand-feet-high summit.

We'd stared at it until the combined rumblings of our stomachs made the other visitors nervous that maybe the active volcano that hid inside the beauty of the mountain might be preparing to erupt. Tan had insisted we eat a bite in the revolving restaurant at the top of the Needle. Once we opened the dinner menu, we'd realized the prices were a little too much for our shoestring budgets. My knight in white cotton had devised a romantic plan—we'd pool our resources and buy one meal to share.

I'd dug in my purse for any bills or change hiding out while Tan did the same in his wallet. We'd been elated when together we had enough to buy a shareable-size appetizer. Mission accomplished, and one of the best dates of my life because we'd made it happen together.

The pleasant memory poked a nerve in my brain and forced me to sit up straight in bed. I sent a text to Agnes. *How much is Chef Jonathan asking you to invest?*

I waited only five minutes before she responded. Guess she hadn't been able to sleep either.

Two hundred thousand. Why?

This was math I could do without a calculator. You didn't have to be smarter than a fifth grader to add Agnes's potential investment to the fifty thousand Jonathan had asked of me to come up with the magic number: $250,000. The exact amount of the blackmailer's demand.

CHAPTER TWENTY

———

My fingers hurt by the time I unlocked the door at Smugglers' Tavern to begin the workday. Between texts to Agnes to reassure her and review the details—for the ten thousandth time—and fielding phone calls from Officer Faria to assure him it was alright to conduct their sting operation on tavern property, I was certain my fingers and mouth would be cramping for the next hour or so.

My stomach still didn't feel well. I'd tried some more of the tea Agnes had given me, but halfway through, the acrobatics of my internal organs forced me to forego any more of the beverage. I debated making myself a hot toddy to help settle myself down. Gram would occasionally mix together a little of her secret stash of whiskey, hot water, honey, and a stick of cinnamon to give me when I didn't feel well. There was just enough whiskey in the ones she'd made to ease the tummy nerves, and the honey and cinnamon calmed my spirit.

I opted against Gram's home remedy. Today was going to be a long day, and I needed all my wits to be on full alert. Instead, I chose green tea with honey and added a stick of cinnamon. Three out of four of the ingredients should help, right? Yeah, I wasn't buying it either.

Clara and Tara looked like they hadn't fared any better than I had last night. This week had been tough on almost everyone here in our little work family. Tanner waved hello as he came in, but otherwise had turned his focus inward. He had a big deadline looming. His was still forty-eight hours away. Agnes and Tara—theirs was tonight.

Tourist season was at its peak, but that didn't stop the regulars from coming in. I always enjoyed seeing a familiar face.

Just after noon, a woman walked in who many of the locals seemed to recognize. They either waved or stood up to speak with her as she made her way to the bar. Because everyone I knew was acquainted with her, I felt like I should know her too. But the brain was not functioning at full capacity, and no memory engrams could be recalled. She appeared to be around the age of Janiece Jordan, someone who had lived in Danger Cove for as long as anyone could remember. Officially I didn't know how old Ms. Jordan was—it wasn't polite to ask. She and my great-grandmother were the best of friends, so I placed her solidly in the senior citizen category, but unsure exactly where she fit in there. The mystery woman had blonde hair that was short and curled slightly around her head. Her smile radiated throughout the room and added warmth along with positive vibes. I might not know who she was, but I instantly liked her.

When she finally arrived at the bar, she took a seat and extended her hand. "Good afternoon, Lilly. May I call you Lilly?"

I shook her hand. Firm grip, but not too strong. Another point in the positive column. "Of course. Only my grandmother was called Ms. Waters."

At the mention of my grandmother, a hint of sadness slid onto her smile. "It was a sad day in Danger Cove when the Waters family left. I'm glad to see at least a part has returned."

"Thank you." I hated that I didn't know her name.

About that time, Clara came out to deliver an order. Her face lit up. "Ms. Ashby, so nice to see you. I haven't seen you around town for ages." She set the food down and came around the bar to give the woman a hug.

"Nice to see you too, dear. I've been holed away in my writing cave working on my next story. Your mother called to check on me and updated me with some of the latest goings-on here. Thought I'd venture out and make sure everything was all right with my girls."

Ms. Ashby looked at me and explained, "Let me formally introduce myself. My name is Elizabeth Ashby. The twins' mother and I are in the gardening club together. I've been in Danger Cove long enough that it's hard not to think of these two as family."

If Drake didn't work out, maybe Ms. Ashby would take over gardening. I bet she knew how to coax the very best from the ground. "Nice to meet you, ma'am."

"Don't let her fool you. She's trying to be modest, but she's a bestselling mystery author. Gardening is a hobby, but we all love the stories she tells." Clara beamed with pride as she shared.

Elizabeth squeezed Clara's arm. "Thank you, dear. Might I trouble you for some tea? I'd like to have a word with Lilly."

"Sure thing." Clara bounded off, happier than I'd seen her in days.

Maybe some of that magic would rub off on me. I confess I was a little nervous about whatever words she might want to have with me.

"Would you like a glass of water or anything else while you wait?"

She shook her head. "No, I wanted to say thank you and offer a few words of advice. May I do that?"

I shrugged. "I have no idea why you would need to thank me, but I'm always open to advice." My grin emerged even though I tried to be respectful and serious. "To be fair, I don't always take the advice I'm given. I always listen though."

Ms. Ashby laughed, a rich sound that upped my peace, love, and happiness factor by at least ten. It was easy to see why people liked her. "Fair enough." Her expression turned serious. "I also checked in on my fellow cat lover and friend, Agnes. I wanted to thank you for being there for her. I fear when I'm in the throes of writing, I lose track of time and people."

"I'm sure it's very exciting work. I can see how you could be completely lost in the process."

She winked. "Yes, you more than others would understand the all-in concept."

I opened my mouth to express my wonderment at how she could know that about me when I hadn't even met her until now. She waved off my unasked question. "All the Waters women are like that. Doesn't take someone who solves mysteries to figure that one out."

She was right. "Fair enough. So how is Agnes? It's been a few hours since we last spoke."

Clara brought the tea and a biscuit with honey out for our guest and placed it in front of her. "Here you go. Enjoy."

"Thank you, Clara. Why don't you stop by after work, and we'll talk?" Elizabeth's comforting voice made me want to take her up on the offer if Clara didn't.

The young woman hung her head. "Depending on what Tara decides, I may not be very good company."

"Which is exactly why you should stop by. I'll regale you with my latest tale before we discuss any personal matters. I have some of that ice cream that you adore. Celebration or commiseration, you can't go wrong with ice cream."

Clara nodded. "Okay, thank you."

Ms. Ashby returned her attention to me after Clara left and answered my previous question. "Agnes is hanging in there. She's resilient. She also said you'd been very helpful and kind to her. I wanted to say thank you for that."

My face heated from my blush, so I grabbed some glasses and rubbed imaginary spots from them. "Just being a friend."

She nodded and then sipped her tea for a moment. "I trust you and the police have taken all necessary precautions to ensure her safety tonight in this little trap you're staging?"

The heat on my face matched the noonday sun outside. You had to appreciate her direct approach. "Officer Faria has assured me they will be close by and will maintain a visual on her." I smiled at the term. "His words, not mine. I'm still nervous, as it's usually only myself that I put in harm's way. Is this where the advice part comes in?"

Her blue eyes twinkled. "No, I trust our police force will provide all the necessary protection. My advice is more in the area of all the puzzles you're trying to piece together to get to the whodunit."

"You'd certainly know about that," I started and then realized how that might sound. "I mean, not that you've actually committed any real crimes…just plotted them…" Ugh, at this rate, I would be the next victim in her new book. Or worse, the killer.

"I do spend a lot of time thinking up reasons why someone might kill another person and how. That is true. I've also discovered that often times we are so focused on the obvious that we miss the truth hiding just below the surface."

"Meaning?"

"You've been focused on the money, right?"

I nodded. "Seems logical. We believe Rico was being blackmailed and now Agnes. Money is a powerful motive for murder."

She ate a few bites of her biscuit and drank some more of her tea as I waited not-so-patiently for her to enlighten me.

"If Rico was going to pay the blackmail, why would someone kill him? He obviously had access to more money. Maybe the ten thousand was a weekly installment rather than a one-time payout."

Point to Ms. Ashby. She now had a commanding lead, but I wanted to at least try to stay in the game. "Alright, let's say that's true. Money is still the only motive that makes sense to me. Maybe that's why they moved on to blackmailing Agnes?"

She finished her biscuit and tea and put some money on the bar. She took my hand and focused her gaze directly onto me. "Killing someone is usually more emotion than logic. Some of the top motivators for murder are anger, jealousy, obsession, revenge, and a host of other emotionally driven reasons."

"You're saying I should look for the illogical?"

My hand was released, and she offered another smile. "Perhaps. It will only seem illogical until all the puzzle pieces are revealed. Once that happens, you will understand. Until then, I'm simply asking you to look beyond that which fits nicely into your gift-wrapped motive box."

I nodded. "I'll do my best. Thank you for your time and advice."

"Thank you for watching over Agnes. I look forward to seeing this story get to the happily ever after." She graced me with one more smile and then left.

She'd given me a lot to think about. I grabbed a napkin from the bar, since my purse with the notebook in it was locked up in the office. I wrote the ideas she mentioned down so I could consider each one and who might factor in.

"Are you writing a note to pass to Tan?" Mandi teased as she handed me a drink order for one of her tables.

"That would be more fun than this." I held up the napkin for her inspection as I started on the drinks.

Her face scrunched up. "Anger, jealousy, obsession, and revenge? What kind of list is this?" She tossed it back in my direction. I didn't blame her—the negative energy in that list was disturbing.

"The kind of list Ms. Ashby gave me as alternative motives to Rico's murder. Any thoughts on who might fit into those categories?" Mandi was a detail person. Maybe she'd see an angle I hadn't.

"Let me deliver the drinks, and then we'll brainstorm."

Now see when she said it, I knew she actually meant brainstorming. Tanner's offer to help me last night was shrouded with ulterior motives—not that I blamed him. My motives were the same.

A minute later, Mandi had returned. She ripped a few pages off the little notebook she used to take orders. A small slip of paper slid out and fell on the floor at my feet. "Here, use this," Mandi offered as she handed me the loose pages. "They're a little more durable than the napkin."

Best. Friend. Ever. Hey, it's the little things that make relationships great. I'd take those any day over grand gestures. "Thanks." I grabbed my pen and leaned over to pick up the dropped paper. I handed it to her. "Any thoughts?"

Mandi blushed when I handed it to her, as the name on the receipt was *The Pelican Bar*. "It's not what you think," she blurted out.

I chuckled. "I wasn't thinking anything...other than about motives for murder."

She sat down. "My dad is still working on winning Mom back. He thought it would be fun to take her there on a date. I told her it was a bad idea, as the clientele there are a little rowdier than here at the tavern."

"How'd you end up with the receipt?" I wasn't accusing her of anything, just curious.

Mandi flipped the notebook closed to show her mom's name written on the front. "I grabbed hers by accident this morning on my way out."

My teenager side emerged. "Anything good in there?"

She tried to feign a surprised look, but I didn't buy it for a second. "What makes you think I would look?"

I crossed my arms and gave her a look that said *Really?*

Her laughter cut through the imitation indignation. "Okay, I looked. Nothing interesting there but the receipt."

My triumphant smile faded. "Rico visited the same bar before he died. Agnes found a receipt when she was looking for the blackmail note before." A part of me worried this bar might become serious competition for Smugglers' Tavern. Maybe I should check out the competition before the dinner rush just to get the vibe of the place. That was what a responsible assistant manager would do, right?

I also remembered Maura saying she and Blake had visited there too. I almost opened my mouth to share my plan with Mandi, but Tan was in earshot. He would fuss at me for going alone. Part of me wished I could bring my BFF with me, but I'd need her to cover for me at the bar.

Mandi's voice broke into my strategizing. "You're going over there, aren't you?"

Lying—or even sugarcoating the truth to avoid a lecture—was out of the question. "I'd ask you to come, but..."

"But you need me to cover for you here."

"I'll check with Clara, Tara, and Drake to see if they need anything. Might as well make the most of my venture." Plus, it would explain my absence to Tan.

Mandi nodded and grabbed my cocktail napkin notes. "Since things are slow right now, I'll try to think of candidates for each of these categories while you're away. Just be back before the dinner rush. You know how much they all love the way you mix the cocktails."

I came around the bar and gave her a quick hug. "Thanks for supporting me and all my trips into Crazy Town."

"You have a good heart, and that's what BFFs are for, right?"

"Right."

The kitchen was eerily quiet when I made my way to the office. Ashley was cleaning out the fridge, and Clara and Tara were finishing up the last of the lunchtime dishes. "Hi, everyone.

I have to run a couple errands. Is there anything you need for dinner tonight?"

Tara shook her head, and the other two didn't respond. Guess that meant they were all set. "I was thinking about bringing back some chocolate treats for the team from Cinnamon Sugar Bakery. Any preference?"

Ashley's face lit up. Nothing like chocolate to ease the stress of the day. "I would love one of those chocolate éclairs."

Her enthusiasm was contagious. Even Clara smiled. "Anything chocolate works for me."

I turned to Tara. "How about you?"

"I'll pass. Thanks, Lilly. My stomach hasn't been cooperating today. I should probably avoid anything sweet."

Just like that the tension returned to the room faster than calories traveled to your hips. I moved over next to her and gestured for her to follow me into the office.

As soon as the door was shut, she started. "I'm sorry, Lilly. I know I'm bringing everyone down. I just can't decide, and it's driving me—and everyone else—crazy."

"Don't apologize. Good Lord knows I drive the people closest to me crazy ninety-nine percent of the time. The trick is you have to deliver results with the craziness."

She grinned. "Like when you catch a killer?"

"I was thinking more like coming up with the perfect signature cocktail each month, but I suppose my little quirks have occasionally helped solve some mysteries. In both cases, do you know what I do?"

Her expression focused, and I could almost see the need for guidance in her intense gaze. Though I wasn't sure my advice was worthy, I shared my thoughts. "I follow my heart. No matter what logic says is the best thing or even the right thing. My heart guides my actions. Even Ms. Ashby mentioned how powerful a motivator our emotions are. At the end of the day, you have to follow your heart. It's the best way I know to find your path in the twists and turns of life."

"I want to, but I'm not sure how."

This was tougher. "My guess is it's different for each person. Try to block out what everyone else wants and listen to that small voice inside of you that knows better than anyone else what Tara wants or needs. Then make your decision."

She nodded. "Thanks. I'll try."

Ironic that I could give such great advice but have a hard time following it—at least when it came to matters of the heart. "There you go. Alright, I'm going to check with Drake before heading out."

Tara opened the door. "Oh, and Lilly?"

I grabbed my purse before looking up. "Yes?"

"I'd like a chocolate croissant. They melt in your mouth."

Her statement along with a small smile made me chuckle. "One melt-in-your-mouth croissant coming up."

The late afternoon sun shone through the trees surrounding the property behind Smugglers' Tavern. I glanced longingly at my favorite bench. It had been a while since I'd been able to come out back and relax. Part of me wondered if I'd subconsciously been avoiding Drake because of the little information I'd gleaned from his background check and the tension in our interactions. Maybe a part of me missed Abe, my previous gardener. Anyone after him would fall short.

I saw Drake emerge from the greenhouse right before I headed in. His features were drawn tight and his brows furrowed. I worried he was having a bad day along with most everyone else on my team. "Everything okay?"

"All good. Something I can do for you?" The concern on his face eased slightly as he responded.

I shook my head. "I'm running a few errands. Wanted to see if you needed anything."

"What I need is for people to stay out of my business."

"Is someone bothering you?" I hoped I wasn't the *people* he was referring to. Talk about awkward.

My words transformed his face into his trademark smile. It was a little scary how quickly his demeanor could change. "Of course not. My mother called. You know how they can be."

I might not know as much as the average person, but I did know. The difference was, I didn't mind. It was kind of nice having my mother snoop around in my business these days. Not wanting to be disagreeable, I nodded. "Yes, they can overstep from time to time. Sorry you're having to deal with that. Other than asking your mother to stay out of your business, is there anything I can get for you in town?"

"No, thanks. I'm going to tend to my flowers and then check the vegetables in the garden. Some of the tomatoes are about ready to be picked."

A gentle breeze blew across my face, bringing with it the smell of fresh herbs. Drake must've just finished working in that part of the greenhouse. For some reason, the smell made me hungry for lasagna. "Fresh BLT sandwiches—my favorite. Thanks, Drake. Text me if you think of anything. I won't be gone long."

"You got it. Now back to my flowers."

I headed to my bike, but before I rode off to investigate the bar, I shot Vernon a text. *Any updates on Drake's background?*

He didn't respond right away. I wasn't surprised. He didn't keep his phone glued to him one hundred percent of the time. Hopefully soon he'd check his phone and get back to me. All these loose ends in my life were starting to cause me a great deal of unrest. At least by the close of business tonight, a couple of matters would be resolved. For better or for worse.

CHAPTER TWENTY-ONE

———

I'd only made it about halfway to The Pelican Bar when my phone dinged with an incoming text. I stopped along the side of the road to see who the message was from. The notification showed Vernon had replied.

No news yet. Be patient.

I fought the urge to remind him that wasn't one of my virtues, but since he was doing me a favor, I'd keep that tidbit of snark to myself. For my gardener though, I was tired of being patient. When I got back to the tavern, I was going to confront Drake about the arrest on his record and get this cleared up once and for all. I should've done it right away rather than relying on someone else to provide assistance. If the last week had taught me anything, it was that there was always the possibility that people would come and go in your life. Being too reliant on someone could leave you high and dry. *And lonely...*

Not wanting to put this off any longer than I already had, I decided my visit to the competition would have to wait for another day. I would stop by the bakery to pick up the goodies I'd promised the girls, along with something for the rest of the team, and then take care of my unfinished business with Drake.

My legs burned from the intense workout I'd given them, but I made it to the bakery in record time. Thankfully, they were still open. My walk was a little uneasy, as my muscles had turned spongy and unreliable. Honestly, with all the bike riding I did, you'd think my calves would be made of stone by now. The universe was totally unfair in this regard.

"Hi, Lilly. What brings you to the bakery this time of day?" Maura called out from behind the display case.

From the lack of pastries on the shelves, it looked like I'd arrived in just the nick of time.

"Been a rough day at the tavern. Wanted to bring some treats in for the team before the dinner rush starts."

She smiled. "Nothing like sugar to lift the spirits. Any particular poison you'd like today?"

Her use of the word poison tickled my senses—and not in a good way. Even though Ms. Ashby had said to look beyond the logical, sometimes there was a method to the madness. Agnes had become ill every time she drank the tea Rico had given her. I'd also not felt well after drinking the other tea he'd gifted her. It made me wonder if her new husband had more specific designs on getting Agnes's money. Perhaps he wanted all of it rather than the little bit she'd allow him access to? I shot off a text to Agnes. *No more of Rico's tea until we can have it tested.*

There was no reply, but my guess was that she was making a rather large withdrawal from the bank. It would be closing time soon, so she'd need to make sure she followed through to make the plan work.

I gave Maura my order and waited for her to fill the bag with tasty treasures. "Can I ask you a question?"

Maura smiled. "Of course."

"How often do you and Blake go to The Pelican Bar?"

She laughed as she closed up the bag and handed it to me. "I think I've gone a few times, but the first couple were only because I was trying to help Blake figure out who was vandalizing his property."

I nodded and continued my questions. "Is the atmosphere and food good there?"

Maura wiped her hands on a nearby towel. "If you're worried that they're serious competition for your place, don't. People go there for an entirely different reason than they would come to Smugglers'."

"Reasons like?"

"Like they want to make deals or arrangements that they don't want anyone else to know or talk about. Everyone minds their own business there—mostly."

Maybe that was where Rico's blackmailer had met him. That was an arrangement, right? My brain felt like a puzzle board with all the pieces scattered around just waiting for me to put them together in the right order. I just needed to find the corner pieces that would provide the framework.

"You okay, Lilly?" Maura's concerned voice filtered into my brain.

"What? Oh, yes. Just trying to solve a puzzle."

Maura smiled. "I have it on good authority that chocolate makes the mind function at a much higher efficiency rate. And if not, you get to douse your disappointment in a mild sugar coma."

I opened the bag and inhaled. Hard to argue with the perfect combination of milk, sugar, and cocoa beans. "Thanks, Maura. The girls will love this."

"I tossed in a chocolate cake donut for Drake. He mentioned those were his favorite the last time we chatted."

"Thanks. I'll be sure to take it to him. Have a great evening. Stop in for dinner tonight, and I'll treat you to our signature drink, a tequila sunset."

"Oh, that sounds good. I'll see if I can make it over there. Thanks!"

Once the goodies were securely fastened in the basket, I headed back to the tavern. My stomach churned slightly in anticipation of my upcoming conversation with Drake. At least I had a donut to serve as a peace offering before we got down to the business of his background. I was greeted with enthusiasm by my kitchen team when they saw the Cinnamon Sugar bag.

"I thought you'd never get back!" Ashley complained as she took her treat.

I might have been offended, but the sparkle in her eye and the little drop of drool in the corner of her mouth told me it was more anticipation than agitation motivating her words.

"You're welcome." Everyone else was a little more patient as they received their snack. Finally, all that was left was the donut for Drake. "I'm going to take this out to Drake. Be back as soon as I can."

"He's not there," Tara advised. "He said he had to run out for supplies."

This man's lack of time management and organization irritated me more than I cared to admit. I had *just* asked him if he needed anything before I left. His answer had been no. Not wanting to share my aggravation with my sugar-sedated team, I smiled. "I'll just take this out and put it on his desk in the greenhouse. Then we'll get ready to for the dinner rush."

"Take your time. We have everything under control here. We'll text if we need anything."

Early evening in Danger Cove normally boasted a beautiful panorama of colors as the sun began its descent. Orange, purple, and red painting over the blue canvas of the sky to bid the daytime a peaceful night. Tonight, though, the weather had turned stormy. Dark clouds covered the painting, hiding the brilliant colors behind a cloak of misty gray. Just as well, it fit my mood as I thought of Drake and all the other upheaval in my life.

I slipped inside the greenhouse. The fragrance of the flowers greeted me and offered sensory soothing. If I didn't know the dinner rush would be upon us in the next fifteen minutes, I'd hang out in here for a bit. Maybe I should take up gardening or at least have a flower garden. Ha! Yeah, that wasn't going to happen. Guess I'd just have to avail myself of this amenity right behind my place of work.

Once at the back of the building, I placed the treat on Drake's desk. My temporary zen evaporated when I saw over a week's worth of trash in and around the can under his desk. Seriously, why couldn't he just put it in the dumpster on his way from the greenhouse to the kitchen? It wasn't even out of his way.

I grabbed a trash bag from the storage cabinet behind his desk and collected the contents both in and around the can. While I was here, might as well check the bins in the other parts of the building. I moved into the area where the herb garden was and noticed dirt on the ground. If I didn't fire him for whatever was hidden in his background, I might have to do it for failing to take care of the area he was responsible for maintaining. Tara and Clara ran such a neat kitchen, I'd never really had to check up on them. Abe, my former gardener, had been meticulous as well. Drake—not so much.

I looked around until I found a small dust pan and brush. The boards on the floor were unforgiving as I knelt to clean up the mess. The light hit the dirt, and I saw something besides brown reflected in the pile. With the utmost care (I worried it might be a colored insect hanging out in the mess as the ground was kind of their home—I was the invader here), I used the bristles on the little brush to separate the dirt to see if I could figure out what I'd seen.

A moment later, my heart turned into a bass drum thumping wildly against my chest. Silver and green flecks decorated the dirt—just like I'd seen in the glass Agnes had been using to clean her ring. Correction—fake ring. It was wildly circumstantial and made no sense at all to even think he might have the ring. But, I reminded myself, they'd never found it either.

Drake wasn't on the premises during the search. He might have hidden it here in the greenhouse later. It was a long shot, like record-setting sniper long shot, but to satisfy my curiosity, I needed to at least look.

There were plenty of good hiding places in here, but since I found the specks in the dirt on the floor, I'd start by looking in the pots on the closest shelf. I looked for soil displacement in each plant until I found one where it looked like the dirt had been recently disturbed. It required a few inhales and slow exhales before I worked up the courage to put my fingers in the pot and dig down to see if something had been buried in a potential luxury apartment complex for bugs.

My centi-senses skittered along the length of my spine when my fingers came in contact with an object that varied in texture from the soil. *Please don't let it be a bug.* Lifting carefully and fully prepared to scream, I retrieved the item.

There, in my now grimy fingers, was the remains of Agnes's fake wedding ring.

CHAPTER TWENTY-TWO

———

The ring lacked its original luster and resembled something a child would get out of a gumball machine, instead of a symbol of luxury and affluence. At least one corner puzzle piece had taken its place in my mind puzzle. Drake had Agnes's ring. That didn't mean he'd killed Rico, though he'd just catapulted to the top of the suspect list in my opinion.

I needed more corner pieces to get a better picture of what had happened that morning. I tried to remember what else Officer Faria had shared with me about the cause of death. It wasn't something sharp or with an edge, like the table, and it had left no residue in the wound. A blunt, smooth object. Yeah, still didn't really narrow down the possible items much.

Since I had the privacy, I might as well take a look around to determine if I could see anything else out of place. I replayed that morning in slow motion, hoping to remember a detail that might not have seemed relevant at the time.

"I'm just going to grab something from the greenhouse— then I'll be on my way." Drake's voice called out to someone.

My delicious chocolate treat from the bakery started churning in my stomach. Finding the ring was only circumstantial, and there were still two key pieces missing: the murder weapon and the motive.

More time to look around and someplace to hide—that was what I needed. I hurried back to the office area and slid under the desk. Sometimes it paid being petite and reasonably flexible. I pulled the chair in and held my breath as I heard the outer door open. Shitzu! I'd left the trash bag and dust pan out in the area. Maybe he wouldn't notice.

My breath caught in my throat and refused to move when he clomped into the room. His work boots peeked under the desk, and I heard him pick up the bag I'd left him with Maura's gift. "Not my birthday yet, but a present is a present."

The paper rattled as he crumpled it. The noise jangled my already heightened nerves. Maybe he'd be in a sugary-sweet mood should he find me hiding out under his desk. It was a hard sell, but I needed to convince myself of a non-violent end to my snooping. I might have had every right to be in here, but my extracurricular activities could spell trouble.

Unable to see anything other than his boots, I focused on listening. Maybe I'd hear something that would help me not only solve this mystery, but get me out of this sticky situation. I ignored the fact that it sounded like he was eating with his mouth open. Not cool. Gram would not be pleased. Crumbs fell around his feet. I'd bet my next paycheck he didn't bother to sweep it up. He tossed the bag to the ground and headed away from me.

My phone buzzed in my pocket. Not super loud, but in the quiet of the office, it resonated like a starting buzzer at a Danger Cove High School basketball game. Or at least how Tan had described that event to me.

The door to the greenhouse opened and shut before I allowed myself the luxury of an exhale. I crawled out from under the desk and caught my knee on a sharp object. Reaching down, my hand found the culprit—a small snub-nosed screwdriver. Great, not only was he leaving trash on the floor, but his tools as well. I slipped the screwdriver into my purse, stood, and allowed myself a moment to stretch before pulling my phone out of my back pocket. I had a missed call from Vernon, followed by a text. He indicated he'd received a message from his guy and would call soon with an update. Finally, some good news.

I made it back to the area where I'd left my mess. I needed to put the ring someplace safe that would allow me to be hands-free while I cleaned up. Even though it was fake, the stone was too big to fit into the pocket of my capris—at least not comfortably. Wanting to get out of there as quickly as possible, I slid my fingers along my neck to lift my gold chain from under my blouse. A moment later, I'd added Agnes's ring alongside my grandmother's wedding ring and the key to my lockbox at home and returned the chain to its proper place.

I allowed myself a moment to smile as I remembered when Tan had discovered exactly where the key remained nestled. He'd laughed and told me it represented the key to heaven for him. I really was going to miss him.

My sweet dream of that moment broke in two with the sound of a slamming door. I looked up and saw Drake leaning against the doorframe. Logistically, this was a problem, as that doorway represented the only path to the exit in the next room. Quickly, I moved my hands behind my back. Hopefully, he'd been focused on my face. Hey, a girl can hope.

"Lilly, what a surprise to see you in here."

"I brought you a gift from Maura. She recalled you enjoyed the chocolate cake donuts and wanted you to have one."

He crossed his arms and smiled. Not a warm, caring, make-you-feel-warm-and-fuzzy kind of smile, more of a cat-about-to-eat-the-canary grin. "It was delicious. Thank you. I didn't realize you were still in here though. Where were you?"

Umm...hiding under your desk like any respectable assistant manager? Not plausible. "I didn't see you either. I must've been admiring your beautiful flowers, and we missed each other."

His gaze traveled from me to the trash can and then back to me, coming to rest on my chest. Wait! My chest? How rude. He moved toward me, and I had to fight the strong urge to put my hands up to defend myself against whatever he was planning to do.

A moment later his plan was revealed when he guided his hand, index finger pointing out, until the tip touched my collarbone. The centipedes moved from my spine straight to my heart, a thousand nerve endings coming to life—and not in a good way. I swallowed hard before I could lift my head to meet his intense stare.

"You have dirt on you. Wonder where that could've come from?" He lifted my necklace until the hidden treasures were revealed. With one quick jerk, he snapped the chain in two, taking possession of the key and rings. He made a show of looking at each item. "Hmm, one of these things is not like the other."

Somewhere in the midst of all the centipedes, I found a penlight of courage in the darkness. "Agreed. One of them is fake. You have any ideas how it came to be in the greenhouse?"

Drake moved a few steps back and chuckled. "I love your moxie. You run headlong into danger without a second thought. You also stock the best tequila around. None of that crap they serve at The Pelican Bar."

That puzzle piece fell into place a few minutes too late. I remembered Maura mentioning she and Blake had seen Drake there. I needed to stall while I tried to fill in a few more blank spots. "You're saying I'm in danger here? I brought your donut in and accidentally knocked one of the pots over. I was trying to clean it up. That's when I found the ring." Sounded plausible. Two-thirds of it was reasonably true. That had to count for something, right?

"And the ring just what? Fell out with the dirt?"

The amusement in his voice annoyed me. Donna Do-Good, my guardian angel, quickly reminded me that now was not the time to share my annoyance. Kind of hated it when she was right.

Knowing it was impossible for me to behave and hold my tongue for an extended period of time, my gaze darted around the room, looking for something that could be used as a weapon. It would need to be close and something, preferably, that wouldn't kill him. My preference—once I found a bad guy—was to hit pause on the playlist of my predicament and bring in the official dispensers of justice. Anything more than that was above my unofficial paygrade.

My search continued as I responded to him. "Okay, fair enough. I might have seen the dirt on the floor and wondered if there was more to the story."

"Based on a little mess, you decided to go digging through my herbs to see if you could find something? That sounds less believable than some of the stories *I've* told over the years to get myself out of trouble."

There it was—official notification that I was in trouble. I'd suspected it all along, but something about having it confirmed by the big man standing between you and safety brought it all home. "I didn't dig through *all* the pots, just the ones that looked like they had misplaced dirt."

"Well, aren't you a little Nancy Drew? Too bad the Hardy Boys aren't nearby to rescue you."

"Who?" I knew who they were, but figured playing dumb could be in my best interest at the moment.

Drake shook his head. Guess I figured wrong, as my pretending to not know upset him even more. I decided I needed to keep fishing. I had enough edges around my puzzle to start moving a few other pieces into place. While I talked, I slid my hand into my purse to retrieve the screwdriver. It wasn't much of a weapon but would be far more effective than my tube of Chap Stick. It also happened to be small enough for me to conceal in my palm.

"You mentioned The Pelican Bar earlier. I feel a little betrayed. Was the bartender over there better than me? Based on what you said earlier, it can't be the alcohol."

At the mention of alcohol, my brain honed in on a favorite of both Agnes and Drake: tequila! Drake had a bottle in here earlier. He was supposed to have taken it home, but I'd be willing to bet Mandi being on the other team in Trivial Pursuit that he hadn't done so yet. Before he could answer, I continued, "Speaking of alcohol, any chance you failed to follow my instructions and take the bottle you had here home? I could use a shot of it about now."

Drake laughed as his gaze darted—for just a second—to the bottle of tequila on the shelf behind me and to the right. I followed his gaze and noticed not one but two bottles of the stuff on his shelf. One bottle was the cheap brand I'd found the other day during my impromptu tour. The other...

A bottle of Tsunatka tequila.

CHAPTER TWENTY-THREE

———

I remembered Agnes had sworn she'd just put a new bottle on her dining room table the afternoon Rico had died. Coincidence? I didn't think so. I decided to poke the bear a bit. I pointed to the first bottle. "I thought we agreed you'd take that home, not bring more in."

Drake moved closer. Not good. "Maybe I have a drinking problem. Too bad for you that little detail didn't show up on my background report."

Fear—real fear—started to tiptoe up my spine. Even the centipedes had fled. Not a good sign. Best-case scenario—Drake had had the misfortune of being at Rico's house when everything went down, and this was a crime of opportunity, where he stole the ring and his favorite adult beverage. Worst-case scenario—he was there because *he* was the killer.

Time for a distraction. I reached down deep into my humor reserves and dredged up the best possible chuckle I could muster. "Either your mom sent you one heck of a birthday gift, or I'm paying you too much if you can afford a bottle of Tsunatka tequila."

Drake was standing right in front of me now. Important bodily functions like heartbeats and breaths suspended as I waited to see what he would do. He reached around me to grab the cheap bottle. Opening it, he retrieved two shot glasses. Pouring a generous measure, he handed it to me. "Sorry, not willing to part with the good stuff for you. I'm saving that to celebrate."

I downed the shot. Hey, cheap, nasty-tasting liquid courage was better than going solo at this point. "Celebrate what?"

He stepped back and returned some of my personal space. My relief was short-lived, though, as a folding chair from the other corner was retrieved along with a pack of zip ties. I didn't care what scenario you were looking at, this was *not* a winning combination. At least not for the person who would have to...

"Sit in the chair."

Yeah, that was what I was afraid he was going to say.

I plastered a smile—totally fake—on my face and backed away a couple steps. My fingers closed even tighter around the screwdriver. I totally could use a Mary Poppins purse about now—or one like Hermione Granger had in *Harry Potter* to secure a bigger, better weapon. But at a time like this, I'd have to work with what I had. "I appreciate the offer, but I'm not tired. Besides, I need to get back inside."

He chuckled. "I'm sure you would, but I think I prefer your company right now. You have a great team. They'll be fine without you."

I wish he'd added *for a bit* or some other indicator that I could get out of here sooner rather than later. My palms were a little sweaty, but I made fists with both hands and prayed he didn't make me open them. Otherwise, my only advantage—the screwdriver—would be lost.

Once seated, he made quick work of securing my wrists together behind my back. Since I wasn't sure what his plans were with me—though I couldn't imagine how they could be good—I opted to play twenty questions. I planned on doing the asking and hoped he would oblige me with answers. It was the least he could do since he'd ensured my continued presence in this unfolding nightmare.

I started by repeating my last question. "What are we celebrating?"

Drake poured himself another shot of tequila and downed it in one gulp. He wiped his mouth with the back of his sleeve and then offered a triumphant smile. "I'm about to get rich. Not so rich to draw unnecessary attention, but enough to keep me in a manner to which I'd like to become accustomed."

Pretty big words and dreams for someone who could barely show up to work on time. Time to call his bluff—just a bit. He did still hold all the cards and the penknife necessary to release these zip ties. "So what number are we talking about? Ten grand?"

Drake laughed and retrieved another chair so he could sit down in front of me. "Ten thousand is chump change. That's the kind of number you ask for when you have someone who has to gain access to money that isn't theirs."

"Like Rico?" I figured, at this point, that Drake's plans for me weren't going to end well. My only hope was to stall him long enough for someone to start to wonder where I was and come looking for me. It was doubtful I could stall him long enough until the police arrived for the sting operation, but that was my goal if help didn't arrive sooner.

He stretched out in the chair, his long legs crossed at the ankles. Totally comfortable and relaxed. "Rico and I grew up in the same area of town. I tried to be a friend to him, but he was always too busy dreaming up his next big con. After a time, I no longer admired him. I was jealous of him. I worked hard to perfect my cons so that one day I would be better than him."

"Why were you arrested?"

The muscle in his jaw clenched. I must've hit a nerve somewhere. Good. He had all my nerves doing a dance. Seemed only fair he experienced a little turmoil as well. "I'd selected a perfect target for my next mark and had been working her all evening when he moved in on my territory."

"And you fought back."

"You bet your best bottle of tequila I did. We both ended up in the same cell overnight for a drunk and disorderly charge. After that, I switched tactics." He grinned a satisfied smile. "Blackmail offers a quicker return on my investment."

More puzzle pieces started to fit together. "You saw Rico and knew he was running a con on Agnes." Not that everyone who had been around any length of time didn't suspect that all was not on the up-and-up for the newlyweds. Didn't take a criminal to figure that out.

"Exactly. I decided time to recoup some of my losses from cons he'd beat me out of in the past. Ten grand every other week. Didn't want to be too greedy. This was more about revenge than restitution. I wanted to make his new wife nervous about the sums he was withdrawing from her account."

Not always about the money. Ms. Ashby had been one hundred percent on target with that advice. "So you went to pick up the blackmail money and what—you argued and it got physical?"

He dragged his long fingers through the black waves of his hair. "I didn't plan to kill him." He paused, brows furrowed. Maybe he was weighing how much to tell me. "Why are you asking me these questions? You have to know if I tell you, there's no way I can let you go."

He made a very good point. "It sounds like it was an accident. I've had a lot of dealings with the police. Maybe if I know everything, I can help you frame the story the best way so the police understand it was an accident too."

Drake laughed. "Do you think I'm an idiot?"

Honestly, what was with everyone making that a go-to comment? I didn't like being called an idiot. I wasn't going to call anyone else that either—especially not someone who held all the power at the present moment.

Before I could respond, he continued. "You live about as far from reality as one can get and still function in this world, don't you?"

I shrugged. "Not the first time I've heard that. So why don't you tell me the rest of what happened that morning? I believe you when you said you didn't plan to kill him. You wanted to make him suffer and show him you had the power." Drake had wanted to knock Rico a couple rungs down on that power ladder.

Drake downed another shot of tequila. Maybe if help didn't arrive soon, he'd be too drunk to kill me.

"I went to pick up the first blackmail payment. When I arrived, Rico was slumped in his chair, unconscious. I'm guessing the fumes were to blame. Agnes couldn't even get the solution right. If she would've followed my instructions, he would have suffered, but no one would've died."

"You're her DIY friend?" It hadn't seemed important at the time to ask Agnes about that detail, as we were dealing with so much other trauma. "I didn't even realize you two knew each other."

"We're not the best of friends, but we ran into each other at The Pelican Bar. Alcohol there isn't as fancy, but it's a good place to fade into the background. She and I are both big fans of tequila, as you know. We like that the bartenders there aren't as nosey."

If I weren't already in danger, I'd be offended. "Must be terrible to have someone care about you." When scared, I spoke fluent sarcasm.

He ignored my comment. "Agnes was whining about Rico and how she was sure he only married her for the money. Of course, she was right, but I wasn't going to confirm it since I wanted him to keep paying me. I suggested adding a little extra ammonia to her cleaning solution to make him suffer a bit if she suspected he wasn't being honest with her. Of course, she didn't mention that she already knew the ring was a fake. Probably how she knew *he* was a fake too."

Drake was probably right, but he wasn't going to hear that from me. I managed to hold any comments so he would continue.

"I saw the ring in the glass, not realizing yet it was a fake, and decided to take advantage of the opportunity. I'd no sooner grabbed the ring, than the jerk woke up. He saw I had the ring and lunged for me."

"He had to know the ring was fake though. Why would he attack you over that? He could've let you go and told her the ring was stolen while he was unconscious."

"Because that son of a..."

He paused and shot me a quick grin as he stopped before cursing. "...called me a loser and said he didn't mind paying 'cause he'd found someone new to con in addition to Agnes, so money wasn't going to be a problem."

"Did he tell you who?" Or maybe that was why Drake had killed Rico—for withholding that valuable information.

His smirk caused the muscles in my gut to tighten another notch or two. How had I not seen his nefarious nature before?

He leaned forward. "Of course he didn't. But I'm smarter than he gave me credit for. Since he's no longer around to execute the blackmail, I'm going to do it instead."

I remembered Allyson catching the use of tenses in my conversation with her and decided to apply that same logic to Drake's statement. I was pretty sure—now—he was the one blackmailing Agnes, so that was past tense. His word choice was *going to.* In my mind that meant he hadn't done it yet. There was only one person that I knew—with a secret and money to pay the blackmail—that Rico, Drake, and I all knew. Another puzzle piece clicked into place. "Chef Jonathan."

Drake's smile added another rock to the pile growing in my stomach. "Pretty smart for a bartender."

I knew I'd discovered Chef Jonathan's secret from having to taste his food, but to my knowledge Drake hadn't partaken and the food Rico ate had actually been prepared by Clara and Tara. "How did Rico find out? How did you find out, for that matter?"

"I'm guessing Rico learned from one of his sources. He made lots of money from his cons and paid well for tips. He ran in circles you and I only dream about. I'm sure one of them tipped him off."

"And you?"

"Sweet, sweet Clara mentioned her suspicions to me while she was sharing her despair over the possibility of Tara leaving. I assured her everything would turn out just fine and to have faith." His expression hardened. "Of course, I have no idea how life will turn out for her. She'll live. The information she provided prompted me to reach out to my contacts. It cost me a pretty penny to learn that the good chef has not only lost his ability to taste, but thanks to nasal polyps, his sense of smell is dwindling too. That will give me the leverage I need to finally break into the big time. No more working for pennies at a bar. No offense."

Gee, how could I take offense to that? Rather than squabble with him over his pay, I wanted to learn what had happened that day at Agnes's. The clock inside my head reasoned that surely someone had missed me by now and had called the police—or at least would come to look for me. I wanted answers before the cavalry arrived. "No offense taken.

So after Rico's confession about the new con, you fought. You were angry. I can understand that, but then what happened? The coroner said he hadn't hit his head on the table."

Drake's gaze traveled to the bottle of Tsunatka tequila. "He didn't. I introduced his thick skull to a brand new bottle of tequila, which his wife had so graciously left on the table. Seems fitting in a way. Agnes hated him. She loved tequila. Love triumphs over evil once again."

My eyes widened. Talk about illogical. Time to wrap up this nightmare. "Once Agnes pays, you're done with her, right? I assume the money Chef Jonathan will pay for your silence will be more than enough to accommodate your new lifestyle."

"I haven't decided yet. I did let her off easy with the amount demanded. No sense leaving money on the table. Her initial payment will get me away from here and settled in a nice place. I may be able to find a way to get her to pay some more. The money from the tasteless chef will provide steady income. He'll make a fortune from his restaurant empire—I plan on sharing in the wealth with him."

Time to bring Drake down a rung or two on the ladder. "Sounds like a great plan, but only one problem."

He leaned forward, invading my personal space more than the aliens in *Independence Day*. "Oh, and what's that?"

"Agnes isn't going to pay the blackmail."

His tanned skin turned a bright Angry Bird red. Tequila-tainted breath washed across my senses as he spoke in a low, threatening tone. "Why wouldn't she pay? I saw her go into the bank earlier."

Time to see if my storytelling would pass a creative writing class. "She reached out to me earlier and said the police called with the cause of death. Neither her fumes nor the table in her house were the murder weapon. She's confident she won't be found guilty—especially since she didn't do it."

I expected surprise, anger, something more than the wide smile that spread across his face. He pointed to the tequila bottle again—the expensive one. "Weren't you wondering why I kept the murder weapon?"

In all fairness, the thought had crossed my mind. He'd buried the ring but left the proverbial smoking gun barely camouflaged behind some potted plants. I shrugged. "Maybe a little curious, but then again, criminals aren't always the sharpest knives in the drawer, if you know what I mean."

"Well, this criminal happens to be sharper than your average utensil. Sit tight. I'll be right back."

With his back to me, I allowed the fear I'd been holding in check under my sarcastic veneer to seep through my mask. Honestly, where was everyone? I knew they were a well-oiled machine, but I had to have been gone minimally for thirty minutes. You'd think at least Tanner would have noticed my absence.

All too soon, Drake returned, and I had to transform back into my reckless, confident self. Fake it till you make it, right? *Hopefully, I made it out alive...*He didn't return empty handed. His latex-gloved hands held the beautiful—and deadly—monkshood flower. This turn of events hadn't factored into any plan I'd envisioned. Certainly not in the plan of how I would die.

"Remember how much you loved this plant?"

I swallowed the peach pit–sized lump in my throat and nodded. "I also remember how dangerous you said it was."

He set the flower down on the floor and pulled off some petals with his protected fingers. "Only dangerous if you touch it to bare skin. Like this…"

My fear rocketed skyward as I felt the satin-smooth petals trail down my arms and onto my bound hands. Almost immediately, a tingling sensation followed in its wake. Not the good kind of tingling either. This was the gut-wrenching, fear-inducing I'm-going-to-die tingling. "Why are you doing this?"

Once he'd covered my upper extremities sufficiently, he reached into my back pocket and retrieved my phone. "What's the passcode?"

It was hard to concentrate while the knowledge that poison was flooding my body filled every conscious thought. I couldn't process his request. My delay angered him, and I watched in horror as he plucked another poison petal from the plant.

"No, wait! Give me a second to think."

He moved the petal in front of my face like a pendulum counting down the time I had left to answer his question. Not helpful. I managed to dig through my terror-laden memory banks and retrieve my four-digit PIN number. "Two four two three."

Drake dropped the petal back into the pot and unlocked my phone. He scrolled through my contacts to reach Agnes. Didn't take very long since the list was alphabetical. Why couldn't her name have been Wilma or something? "I'm going to dial her number and put her on speaker. I want you to tell her that plans have changed, and she needs to bring the money now and put it by the door of the greenhouse."

"Don't you think she'll find that suspicious?" Nausea began to brew in my stomach. I wasn't sure if the cause was nerves or the poison. Either way, I prayed I didn't throw up.

"If the cops show up with her, you are going to spend a lot more quality time with the pretty purple plant."

Message received loud and clear. I prayed that the cops, who were already planning on being here later, would demonstrate a superior level of stealth. "Okay. I'll be convincing."

The phone rang several times before she picked up. "Hi, Lilly. I hope you're calling to calm me down. I'm more nervous than a long-tailed cat in a room full of rocking chairs."

Despite the gravity of my situation, I couldn't help but let a small chuckle escape. "Nice analogy, Agnes. Listen, why don't you go ahead and bring the money now. You can put it over by the greenhouse. No one goes out there this time of night. Text me once you've made the drop, and then I'll keep the money safe until the appointed time. That way you won't be in harm's way. I wouldn't forgive myself if something bad happened to you." I was also not going to forgive myself if something worse happened to me.

There was a long pause. "Are you sure?"

Here was my one and only chance to get a message to Agnes in the hopes she'd understand. "As sure as I am that Charlie likes Italian food and tequila." Truthfully, it wasn't much for her to go on, but it was all I could manage with the numbness slowly working its way through my body. "Just trust me, Agnes." I couldn't even add the part about there being a smuggler in the tavern, which was code amongst our team for *There's trouble. Call the police.*

She was quiet for several long, gut-wrenching seconds. I didn't want to think about how much more of the flower Drake would expose me too if I couldn't convince her. Maybe your entire body going numb would prove a painless way to go.

"Okay, Lilly. I'll get everything together and head over there now."

"Great. Thanks. Just trust me it will all work out."

Drake cut the connection before either Agnes or I could say anything further. "Glad to see you're capable of behaving. Detective Marshall doesn't seem to think so based on what I've overheard."

"Yeah, well, he's not at the top of my favorite-people list either." Guess being poisoned didn't change how I felt about that particular member of the force. Though I'd be mighty happy to see him about now, even if he did fuss at me.

Drake returned to the chair opposite of me. He leaned forward and patted my knee. "Don't worry, Lilly. It will all be over soon."

That was what worried me most.

CHAPTER TWENTY-FOUR

———

Time was a fickle thing. If you were having fun, twenty minutes could feel like five. If your life was hanging in the balance, those same minutes felt like hours. I prayed the delay only meant Agnes had picked up on my coded message and knew that Drake was the blackmailer. The plan we'd formed was still the same—just the timing had changed. I prayed that asking her to shorten the time frame would still allow the plan to work and that my message would be interpreted as me being in danger—grave danger. I stopped that line of thinking. Anything that mentioned a grave needed to *not* be in my thoughts right now.

I watched Drake pacing between my position and the door. "What's taking her so long?"

"You kept the bottle to frame Agnes, didn't you? Why would you do that? If she paid you the money, you would have what you wanted."

He stopped pacing and returned to the seat in front of me. "You're so naïve and beautiful. You only see the good in people."

Which was about to get me killed, but no sense in bringing that up. "You're right. I do believe there is good in everyone." Though Drake Butler was challenging that notion with each life lesson he tried to teach me.

"You don't understand how a con works."

I tried to shrug, but I wasn't sure the muscles got the message from the brain. Another wave of nausea rolled through my body. I realized that if I was going to do anything to change the outcome of this night, I needed to act quickly—or I wouldn't be able to act at all. "You're right. I don't."

He pointed to the bottle, which was still sitting hidden among some of the plants closest to the room with flowers…the room with the exit. "I was wearing gloves—occupational hazard of a gardener. You take Agnes's prints and a little of Rico's DNA on the bottle, and that equals the perfect opportunity to frame her for the murder. They won't have any trouble figuring out motive or opportunity with her."

My phone buzzed with an incoming call. Drake looked at it. "Why would Vernon be calling you? Isn't he Ruby's significant other?"

"He's a retired schoolteacher. I called him about putting in a good word for Tanner." Well, the part about having been a schoolteacher was true as far as I knew. I suspected there was more to that story than he'd ever tell me. He had a lot of law enforcement contacts for someone in education. Either that or he worked only with troubled kids.

"Don't answer it."

I started to lift my bound hands and make a sarcastic remark, when I realized that I still *could* lift my hands. I had no idea how long before the poison rendered me unable to move or the nausea made me sicker than Rico's tea. *Or killed me…*I made a show of trying and then managed to summon a few tears. That was the good thing about denying your tear ducts' release all the time—you had a good amount of waterworks in reserve. "I couldn't answer even if my hands weren't bound." I added a sniffle at the end for good measure.

A hint of remorse flashed across Drake's face. I still believed there was some good buried way down deep in him. I lowered my head in mock defeat. "Do you think…"

Drake lifted my chin with his weathered hand. "What? Do you need some water? You have to believe I didn't want it to come to this. I really did like you, Lilly. You gave me a chance when very few people had."

And this was how he repaid me? Felt like people died unintentionally a lot around him. I locked the anger and sarcasm down in a vise of steel. There would be time for that later. I blinked a couple times, sending a few more of the reserved tears down my cheeks. "Then maybe you could repay my kindness by untying me. It's not like I can get away, and Agnes will be here with your money soon." At least I prayed she would.

Conflict covered his stubbled face, but after a lengthy pause, the zip ties were removed. I stood and continued through with the act and pretended to stumble a bit. "Sorry. Happens when I'm in the same position too long." Didn't want to oversell the effects of the poison since he hadn't put any on my lower extremities.

He pointed to the chair. "Sit back down. I don't want you trying to make an escape." The humor in his voice pistoled me off, and I had to tighten the vise on my wayward words.

"You've won. I'm not going to escape—thanks to the pretty purple flower of poison. Agnes will be dropping the money off any minute now. You'll soon be on your way to the riches and freedom you've dreamed of." *And it only cost two people their lives.* Hey, internal monologue can't be controlled. No one is *that* good.

Since his gaze was focused fully on me, I let mine drift to the flower I'd been admiring earlier. "Since you won't let me up, would you at least bring the Stargazer to me? I'd like to smell it again. It was one of my favorites." My hands were folded in my lap. I wanted to be sure when he got to say hello to my little snub-nosed friend, he would be taken completely by surprise. My weapon was small, but I intended to make every inch count.

I heard rustling outside the door. I could only pray that meant help was close by and within hearing range. Since the only prints on the bottle were Agnes's, I needed to try to get him to confess to what I hoped were witnesses outside the door. I would be happy to tell the police or a court about Drake's confession to me—assuming I was around to tell my story—but that would be my word against his. Though one would think my word would carry more weight, I wanted him to pay for all he'd done to my friends and me. I took a deep breath and hoped my voice was loud enough—but not too loud—so that whoever was out there would know to listen. "I know you said you didn't plan to kill Rico, but do you feel any remorse? Any at all?"

Drake laughed. "Not one bit. I played second fiddle to that scammer my whole life. He knew the risks."

He moved closer, and I fought valiantly against the desire to flee. I needed him close.

His hand cupped my cheek. "Though I do regret what I have to do to you."

Agnes's voice cut into his little Machiavellian moment. "I'm just going to set the bag right here by the door, officer. Just like Lilly instructed."

Drake's eyes widened in surprise and anger. I used one hand to grab his neck in an effort to hold him close. With one Herculean effort, I begged my nerves to rise above the poison-induced atrophy and give us one last hurrah. I swung the other hand hard with the intent of putting the screwdriver in as many places on Drake's body as possible before my arm either gave out or he recovered from the initial shock and finished me off. His bicep felt the stab first.

"You bitch!"

My attack caused him to release his hold on me. Deciding escape was better than inflicting more damage to him, I lunged toward the door, the momentum making me fall to my knees. "Help me!"

The door busted open, and my heroes, Officer Faria and Tanner, rushed in amongst other uniformed officers. Faria went straight to Drake while Tanner rushed to my side. He lifted me gently to rest my head in his lap. All of the activity and fast pumping of my blood ramped up the effects of the poison.

"Lilly! What's wrong?"

"Poison—monkshood." I guess if I had to die, doing so in Tan's arms wasn't the worse thing. Of course, if I threw up all over him first, that would ruin the whole tragic love story angle. No one would make a movie with that in the scene.

Detective Marshall stepped through the door and double-checked to make sure his team had Drake under control before he squatted down beside me. He pulled a handkerchief from his pocket and wiped the sweat from my face. Must be another unpleasant side effect of the poison. Fantastic. My voice didn't carry its usual strength. "Tell me you heard his confession. He was wearing gloves…"

"You can tell the detective the rest of the story later." Tan looked up at the non-poisoned people in the room. "She needs an ambulance right away!"

The worry in his voice made me feel even worse than I already did. Once again I'd managed to put myself in harm's way. In all fairness, this time I hadn't done it intentionally.

Detective Marshall responded, "Already done, Mr. Montgomery. Anytime Ms. Waters is involved, I assume extra police and medical attention is required."

Wasn't he the funny one. In an unusual act of compassion, the detective patted my shoulder. "We heard everything. I'd lecture you about getting involved, but I'll save that until you're up and able to argue with me." He offered a small smile. "It's more fun that way."

He turned and nodded to Faria, who made my day with his statement. "Drake Butler, you're under arrest for the murder of Rico Iglesias."

I smiled at Detective Marshall as the darkness crept across my body, lulling me into the bliss of unconsciousness. "Then it's official."

"What's official?"

"The Butler did it in the dining room with the tequila bottle."

He must've picked up on my vague Clue reference since he shook his head and laughed. "Even on the brink of passing out, she finds a way to taunt me that she figured it all out first."

The tingling and numbness moved through my body at an alarming rate, and I prayed that passing out was all I did. I slipped my hand into Tan's and answered the sweet call of darkness.

CHAPTER TWENTY-FIVE

———

Bright, artificial lights greeted me when I managed to open my eyes. Mandi's smile was the first to greet me. "Morning, sunshine. How are you feeling?"

I took a moment to do a quick assessment. "My head is filled with cement, my stomach has churned at least five pounds of butter, and my arms are limp noodles. Does that answer the question?" I softened my complaining with a smile and added, "And I'm incredibly happy to be alive and able to feel everything my body is enduring."

She took my hand and squeezed. "I'm incredibly happy you're alive too."

"What happened? What made Agnes mention the police when she was leaving the money?" Don't get me wrong—I was grateful she did, as that allowed me to act before things got even worse than they already were.

"Agnes was in the tavern when you called."

"What? Why was she there?"

Mandi laughed. "You do recall she'd run out of tequila at her house. With everything going on, she didn't have time to run to Seattle to restock. It's not like they keep that stuff in any of the local liquor stores."

"Touché."

Mandi pulled a piece of paper out of her purse and put it in front of my nose.

"What is that? Smells like an Italian restaurant."

Mandi's smile warmed me to my core. "It's the blackmail note that was given to Agnes. She happened to get a whiff of it at some point and recognized that the smell reminded her of Jonathan and Drake. She suspected one of them might be the culprit. When you called and mentioned Charlie liking Italian food and tequila, we agreed it had to be Drake."

I squeezed her hand. "You are so very good at puzzles. I'm glad you were there to help her."

"You know I love a good puzzle. So I called Officer Faria and explained the situation. The police mobilized sooner rather than later. They figured they would be able to arrest him for kidnapping, unlawful detainment, amongst other things, but…"

"But to get him for murder, they would need more."

"Right. Detective Marshall came up with the plan for Agnes to make her way up to the greenhouse with Faria close behind and with backup nearby. He told them to listen quietly to see if they could overhear anything. Everyone believed you would do everything you could to get Drake to talk." She smiled. "And you did."

I thought of how scared I was at the end, truly believing I was going to die. "You all know me too well. Though, to be honest, this might have been the most scared I've ever been."

Mandi's gaze narrowed. "I can't even imagine how terrifying the whole situation was. I'm so glad you're okay. Thankfully, Drake is behind bars, and you're going to be around to make us smile, mix cocktails, and solve more mysteries."

I nodded but didn't say anything. For some reason, this brush with death had reached down to my innermost being and frightened me more so than ever before. It wasn't the idea of dying. It was more the idea of dying having never truly shared my life with someone else—or even allowed the possibility.

"If you're up to it, there's someone here to see you."

My heartbeat increased its pace in anticipation of who I suspected it might be. "Tanner?"

"Allyson."

The breath escaped in a long sigh that slumped my shoulders, and I closed my eyes. "Oh, okay. You can send her in."

Mandi's hand on my shoulder brought my gaze to hers. Her understanding smile reached through my disappointment. "Tan insisted on handling things at the tavern so I could be here with you until your mom is able to make it in. He wanted to be here."

"What day is it?"

"Thursday."

Tanner had to give his answer to the school by tomorrow. The clock was ticking, and I was laid up in bed. Not good. "Go back and help him. I'll be fine. Ask him if he'll take his lunch break at my place tomorrow afternoon. I want to give him his graduation present."

Mandi giggled. "Gee, I wonder what that could be."

I firmed up my noodle arms and managed to give her a light tap on the arm. "Don't be sassy. I'm not in fighting form. For your information, I plan on cooking lunch for him as part of his gift."

She leaned over and gave me a hug. "I'll ask him to make plans to stop by. Let me know if you need any help with the cooking. I know that's not normally your thing."

"I'll be fine, but thanks for the offer."

The look on her face shared her disbelief that I was capable of cooking a meal for anyone. It wouldn't be a Tara-level meal, but added to the gift I wanted to give Tan, it should do the trick.

Once Mandi left, Allyson came in. "How are you feeling?"

I skipped all the detail I'd provided Mandi. "Happy to be alive. Who knew something so delicate could be so poisonous."

Allyson nodded. "I'm glad Drake is behind bars. I hated Rico, but never wished him dead."

The fact he manipulated, conned, and blackmailed people could inspire a certain level of hate, no doubt. "How are you and Jonathan?"

Her visage brightened at the sound of his name. "We're good. We had a long talk and worked through everything. We're going into business together. Well, my aunt will be involved too. Food and fashion—two things that never go out of style."

"I'm happy for both of you. What about his…illness?"

Allyson's smile dimmed a few watts. "We're looking into surgical options and remain hopeful he'll regain his sense of taste, but he has a trusted sous chef that's been with him for years. He's going to promote him and let him handle the kitchen. Jonathan will have input on what's on the menu, but leave the creation of the dishes to him."

A small ray of hope filled my heart. "Does that mean Tara…"

Allyson chuckled. "Turned him down. She said Danger Cove is her home, and she's not ready to leave. She mentioned something about the closeness of a small town that she didn't want to give up—at least not yet."

I did nothing to hide my sigh of relief. One down, one to go.

Allyson continued. "I also want you to know that Agnes invested the money Jonathan needed even after he came clean about his health issues. He shared his strategy with her, and she agreed with the plan he laid out. You're still welcome to invest if you like. We'd certainly love having you as a silent partner."

Ha! She didn't know me at all if she thought I could be silent about anything. "Thanks, but I think I'm going to invest in my future. You and Jonathan are going to be just fine."

Allyson nodded. "I told him there was no way you'd agree to the silent part. Anyway, we're headed back to San Francisco tonight, but I wanted to say thank you for not using the knowledge you had about Jonathan against him."

"That's not who I am." Curious, reckless, and commitment phobic more accurately described who I was rather than manipulator. I had no desire to enter that power struggle.

"I know, but still wanted to say thanks."

"You're welcome. Best of luck to you and Jonathan in the future."

She nodded. "You too, wherever life may take you."

As she gathered her purse and jacket, I thought about where life was taking me. I'd managed to beat the odds and escape death. It brought into sharp focus that life was short and there were no guarantees. I'd been given a second chance and didn't want to blow it.

She reached down, took my hand, and squeezed. "Goodbye, Lilly. Try to stay out of trouble."

Like that was going to happen.

* * *

Twenty-four hours later, I smoothed my dress for the thousandth time. Why was I so nervous? After being released from the hospital, I'd called to check on everyone at the tavern and let them know I'd be back in to work tomorrow. Tanner had asked to come over after work, but I told him that I was working on his graduation gift and I wanted it to be a surprise when I gave it to him. We briefly talked about the events at the greenhouse. I was grateful he was supportive and didn't fuss at me. In all fairness, this time I'd stumbled into the middle of the hornet's nest, rather than walking toward it with purpose.

Agnes had also called to check on me. She wanted to thank me for helping her through this mess and for the heads-up about the tea. The test showed the tea had been tainted with poison from a hydrangea plant. Nausea, vomiting, and weakness were symptoms. Her thought was Rico had wanted her feeling sick all the time, so she'd be more dependent on him. Guess we'd never know for sure.

I'd also called my mom to fill her in—the abbreviated version—and assure her I was fine. I had to promise to call her every day for the next week to check in so she would know I was okay. It would be a pain, but I kind of liked having her fuss over me.

Once that was done, I'd headed to the store and picked up the items necessary to make Tanner's meal. I double-checked the items in the pan on my stove. It was the first time I'd used both a skillet and a saucepan for one meal. Yeah, totally grown-up now. Okay, making progress on the grown-up, domestic front is more realistic. This meal had sentimental value, which I hoped Tan would appreciate.

I jumped at his knock on the door. Two in the afternoon exactly. Right on time, that was my man. I opened the door and drank in the sight of my lunch date. Black jeans, white T-shirt, and a fake tie clipped on the collar.

"I didn't overdress, did I?"

I laughed. "You're perfect. Love the tie."

"Well, I had to work with what I could manage on my lunch break. My boss has been out sick due to a brush with death, so I've been covering for her at the bar. I know she likes these jeans. The shirt, well, you know I always keep a spare. The tie Ashley helped me find in a box somewhere—a prom leftover."

"You look fantastic. Come on in. Lunch is ready."

He stepped in but then stopped when he took in the table setting with a candle in the middle. His gaze traveled to the stove. "You cooked?"

"Yes. I told Mandi to let you know I was making a meal."

Tan laughed. "I thought that meant you'd order and pick up the food." He looked at the table again. "You really cooked?"

Now I was nervous. "Well, don't get your expectations too high. It could be a long fall down from that pedestal. Shall we sit before it gets cold?"

He nodded. "Sure."

After he sat down, I put the food on our plates and then joined him at the table. I heard the rumbling in his stomach. "What is this? It looks delicious."

"That was part of my plan. Make you wait until two for lunch, so you'd be starving. I know you can stomach anything when you're hungry."

"Very funny." He reached across the table and took my hand. "I can't wait to eat this, not because I'm hungry, but because you made it. That means a lot to me."

Those darn tears started rising to the surface. I thought there might have been residual poison in my system, lessening my control. In order to avoid crying in front of him, I returned to his question. "Well, that's mac and cheese, no big surprise there. I can boil water. The rest was following the instructions."

He smiled. "And the sandwich?"

"Gram called them specialty sandwiches. They were her favorite comfort food. You fry an egg, making sure the yolk is broken and fried along with it, pick your favorite deli meat and warm it on both sides, then top with cheese. Put them all together on toasted bread with mayo, and voila, you have a specialty sandwich. I used sliced turkey. Hope that's okay."

"It's more than okay. It's perfect. Thank you for this wonderful gift."

"You should try it before you dole out too much gratitude. It has been a while since I made them. Gram and I had a lot of happy memories over those sandwiches. Making them after she died was too painful, but I figured it was time."

I watched as my handsome not-boyfriend took his first bites of my culinary creation. As he'd promised, he chewed slowly and seemed to savor each bite. I nibbled on mine. Not because it wasn't good, but because I was still nervous about giving him his gift. Once he'd finished half the sandwich, my lack of patience won out. "Are you ready for your graduation gift?"

He wiped his mouth and smiled. "I thought this fantastic meal was it."

"This—" I gestured to the food. "Was a thank you for not fussing at me for getting involved and putting myself, even if it was unknowingly, in danger again." I reached under the table and pulled out a gift-wrapped box. "This is for your graduation. I'm so proud of you. And no matter what you decide about the job in Chicago, the gift remains yours."

He ripped at the paper and lifted the top off the box. I should've had my phone out to capture a picture of the confusion on his face.

He held up a toothbrush and an empty key ring that had a red Mustang charm on it. "Umm, thanks, Lilly. This is great."

"The toothbrush is for when you spend the night. You won't have to worry about bringing your own."

He blushed. "Oh…"

I grinned. "And the key ring is for your key to whatever place I find when my lease expires. I reached out to Blake late yesterday evening, and he's going to start looking for a small place I can call my own."

Tanner dropped my carefully planned gifts, stood, and moved to my side of table. He pulled me into a hug. "Thank you so much, Lilly. I promise we're still going to take it slow, but just knowing you're willing to move forward—that's the real gift."

I gave up trying to fight the tears and let them trickle down my rosy cheeks. "The offer stands even if it's only when you come home for a visit from Chicago. You were patient and let me follow my path. I'm going to do the same for you. If you go, I'll be here waiting for you when you come home. I just wanted you to know that I'm ready to call Danger Cove my home."

The feel of his soft lips against mine assured me I'd made the right choice. I pulled him closer into my embrace and relished the joy of being alive and, dare I say, in love. A girl could get used to this. No matter what choice Tan made, I was confident in the fact I had made the right one.

Life was good, and I couldn't wait to see what new adventures would be waiting for me around the next turn. I pulled back slightly, much to Tanner's disappointment. I offered a slight smile. "There's one more thing I want to tell you. I…" I needed to say the words and prayed they wouldn't come out sounding anything but sincere and from the depth of my still-a-little-scared heart. "I love you."

Tanner smiled and pulled me close again. "I love you too."

EPILOGUE

Friday. My first day back to work after my latest adventure. There was a lot of catching up to do, so I'd arrived very early. I sat down at Hope's desk with a steaming cup of tea ready to catch up on paperwork, pay bills, and try to come up with a new specialty cocktail. I'd had enough trouble with tequila to last a lifetime.

There were two envelopes on my desk, both with my name on them, but different handwritings. The first looked to be Tanner's handwriting. My gut clenched as I realized this was most likely his resignation letter. I knew I'd told him his decision wouldn't change anything between us, and that was mostly true. Still, my heart sagged at the thought of him leaving. Drawing a deep breath in and exhaling slowly, I opened the envelope.

Lilly,

Please accept this letter as a request to cut my hours to weekends only. I've accepted a job in the Seattle school system teaching fifth-graders. It's the perfect opportunity for me and allows me to remain close to my home in Danger Cove with my family and friends.

If you need to find someone to replace me, I'll understand (at the tavern only, not as your boyfriend—that's right—I'm official now.) No more not-boyfriend status for me.

Otherwise, I'll be happy to train someone to work through the week and then help you out on the weekends. Just let me know your decision.

All my love and respect, Tanner

I folded the letter and held it close to my heart. He was going to stay. He'd make a great teacher, molding young minds and teaching them to be responsible just like he always was.

Before I could open the next envelope, the phone rang. "Smugglers' Tavern, this is Lilly."

"Hi, Lilly, it's Hope. How are you?"

For the first time, I wasn't worried that she'd called to fire me. Not going to lie—it felt pretty good. "I'm doing great. How are you?"

"I've never been happier, and I have you to thank for that—at least in part. You've been doing a great job running things there."

I blushed, mostly because she obviously hadn't been brought up to speed by Ruby on my latest hiring fiasco. "I'm trying, but finding a gardener has been tough. The last one…"

Hope laughed. "Is in jail."

Okay, maybe Ruby had brought her up to speed. "Yeah, he's in jail. You wouldn't think it would be that hard to find someone, but it has been. I'm starting the search again today."

"You'll find just the right person. Trust the universe to guide you. I know it's been guiding me to my latest decision. I hear you were approached about investing in a restaurant in San Francisco."

The fun nature of the conversation flip-flopped, taking my stomach with it. "I never seriously considered it."

"Relax, Lilly. I want to make you an offer to invest in a different restaurant."

My mind scrambled trying to figure out where Hope was headed with this. I should've drunk more tea before I had answered the phone. "Oh? Where?"

"I want you to become part owner of Smugglers' Tavern. I can't let her go completely—it holds a special place in my life and led me to so many wonderful people and things. I would be more of a silent partner. You could still call for advice, but we'd own it together. I've asked Attorney Pohoke to draw up some papers for you to review. How much you invest will depend on your percentage of ownership. I'm offering up to fifty-one percent if you want it."

I didn't know what to say—literally.

"Lilly? Are you still there?"

Her words brought me out of my whirlwind of thoughts. "Yes, I'm still here. Thank you so much for believing in me and for this opportunity."

"Thank you for giving me the chance to pursue my path to happiness while still holding on to the joy of my past. Once you've had a chance to review the papers, call me with any questions, and we'll talk. Okay?"

Me. Part owner of Smugglers' Tavern. What couldn't be okay with that? "Sounds good. Tell Harvey I said hello."

"Will do. Give everyone there a hello for me as well."

I'm not sure how long I sat there after I hung up. Life was changing and quickly, but it didn't scare me like it did before. Maybe that meant I was growing up. I took another sip of my tea. It had gone cold. Guess I'd been sitting here for a while, dreaming of what my new future might look like.

Enough dreaming for now though. Time to get back to the paperwork at hand. I opened the next envelope and pulled out a newspaper. It was a paper from Chicago. The headlines read that the Giovanni family crime syndicate had ended. Giovanni senior had died of an illness, and sources said that testimony provided by a number of key witnesses led to enough arrests of the senior members to leave the once strong dynasty in crumbles.

This had to be a message from Abe, my former gardener and friend. Maybe this meant he might be free to pursue a normal life again. Only time would tell. One thing was certain— if he returned to Danger Cove, the job of gardener was his.

I heard a knock on the door and looked up to see Tanner standing there looking happy as ever. He had a bag from the Cinnamon Sugar Bakery. "I brought a cinnamon scone to celebrate my new job. Care to share it with me?"

"You mean you only brought one?" I stood and made my way over to him. "I'll have you know that I deserve the whole scone, even if you are the one who got a new job."

He pulled out the scone and handed it to me. It was still warm. I truly was a lucky girl to have him in my life.

"Why do you deserve the whole scone if I'm the one we're celebrating?"

I allowed myself a couple of bites before I gave him a crumb-filled smile. "Because I have to find a new security guy and gardener."

"As long as he's not too cute. I won't be having my girlfriend distracted by eye candy while she's trying to do her job."

I hugged him tightly. "You're the only eye candy I'm interested in, pretty boy."

The warmth of our embrace sealed in my happiness. There was one thing I needed to know though before I let go. "You didn't turn down the job because of me, did you?"

"No. The opportunity in Seattle gave me room to grow and learn more, along with a nice benefits package. It also had the advantage of giving me the best of both worlds. Being able to pursue my new career and still be close to my family. I think you and I both have learned how important family is. I don't want to be that far away from mine or..." He lifted his head from my shoulder to look into my eyes. "From the people I care about."

I kissed him and allowed myself to get lost in the happiness of the moment. It would be a change, but life was about change and growing with the ups and downs that were sent your way. Plus, it would still allow us to ease into this next phase in our relationship. The perfect solution.

Tanner ended the kiss. "Guess I need to get started on my workday. Don't want to get fired before my new job starts."

"That was a great kiss, but you're still not getting the scone."

He laughed and pulled another one out of the bag. "Always prepared, I am. Do I know my girlfriend or what?"

"Indeed you do. Now let me finish this treat and my work before I have to report to the bar. I have new employees to hire and a new cocktail to create."

Tanner blew me a kiss and left me to get back to my work. Once I'd wrapped up the necessary paperwork, I walked through every area of the tavern, slowly assimilating the fact that I could be part owner of this wonderful establishment that had come to mean so much to me.

One thought stood at the forefront of my mind as I soaked everything in: tomorrow might not be promised, but today—life was good.

ABOUT THE AUTHORS

Nicole is the *USA Today* bestselling author of the contemporary romance series, *Heroes of the Night*. She has been an avid reader and lover of books from a very young age. Starting with Encyclopedia Brown, Nancy Drew, and Black Beauty, her love for mysteries grew and expanded to include romance and suspense. A Midwest girl, born and raised, her stories capture the love and laughter in her real world heroes and heroines.

Visit Nicole online at: http://www.nicoleleiren.com

USA Today bestselling author Elizabeth Ashby was born and raised in Danger Cove and now uses her literary talent to tell stories about the town she knows and loves. Ms. Ashby has penned several Danger Cove Mysteries, which are published by Gemma Halliday Publishing. While she does admit to taking some poetic license in her storytelling, she loves to incorporate the real people and places of her hometown into her stories. She says anyone who visits Danger Cove is fair game for her poisoned pen, so tourists beware! When she's not writing, Ms. Ashby enjoys gardening, taking long walks along the Pacific coastline, and curling up with a hot cup of tea, her cat, Sherlock, and a thrilling novel.

Visit the official
Danger Cove 🗼

website!

We're a sleepy little town in the Pacific Northwest and home to renowned mystery novelist, Elizabeth Ashby. Don't let out name fool you—we are the friendliest (if deadliest) small town you'll ever visit!

Meet the local residents, explore our interactive town map, and read about the next Danger Cove mystery!

www.dangercovemysteries.com

If you enjoyed *Tequila Trouble*, be sure to pick up these other Danger Cove Cocktail Mysteries!

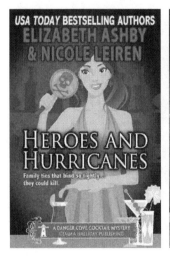
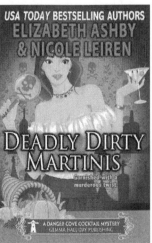